The
White Dove

Lois Thompson Bartholomew

HOUGHTON MIFFLIN COMPANY

BOSTON 2000

The text of this book is set in 12.5-point Dante.

Library of Congress Cataloging-in-Publication Data

Bartholomew, Lois Thompson.
The white dove / by Lois Thompson Bartholomew.
p. cm.
Summary: Having escaped from the compound where she was
imprisoned by the usurper of her dead father's throne, Tasha fights
to survive while planning how to join those working to turn the
kingdom into a democracy.
ISBN 0-618-00464-5
[1. Adventure and adventurers—Fiction.] I. Title.
PZ7.B2812957wh 2000
[Fic]—dc21
99-33517
CIP

Manufactured in the United States of America
HAD 10 9 8 7 6 5 4 3 2 1

To my family, with love and thanks.

AUTHOR'S NOTE

THE KINGDOM OF COMNOR DOES NOT EXIST. DO NOT try to find it, even in disguise, among any of the nations of the earth. It, like Prydain, Tatooine, and Narnia, is a place of the imagination. As an imaginary country, it has its own history that is likewise not tied to the history of any earthly country.

The White Dove is a story of the imagination, but it is not a fantasy. There is no magic in this book, no speaking trees, no wizards, no spells or flying carpets. The only magic in *The White Dove* is the magic that lies within each one of us. It is the strength and courage we find when we discover a goal worth working for, a cause worthy of sacrifice.

I

"THE OLD MAN, HE WANTS TO SEE YOU AFTER SUPPER."

Tasha looked up. The leering face of the serving woman leaned closer. "Perhaps now you will have more than a sickly child to keep you warm."

Tasha turned her head, repulsed by the thought and by the stench of the woman's breath. The old servant moved on, sliding hot bowls of soup onto the table with an ease born of years of practice. Tasha felt hot anger boil up within her.

"What impudence!" she thought, "Didn't he know?"

There was a gentle tug at her sleeve.

"Look, Tasha, we have meat again." Raina's wide eyes were shining with the happiness of the unaccustomed treat.

They had had meat often in the two months since the old man arrived—a bit of rabbit, a taste of squirrel, even fish. Now, tonight, the soup was rich with hearty chunks of venison.

Tasha looked up to find the old man's eyes upon her, clear and honest. Somehow they reminded her of her father's eyes. "Piercing blue," Marko would have said. She felt the hot flush of shame in her cheeks, shame for the old woman's thought and for her own anger. She had nothing to fear from this man.

Often after supper, as she had sat with the other workers huddled around the fire for warmth, she had felt those eyes upon her. He had never joined the others. His chair was in the shadow by the chimney, where he sat carving a stick of wood. Though she could never see his face, when the knife would pause in its flashing, she knew he was watching her and the child.

Tonight she moved her chair to the end of the semicircle. It was colder here than in the middle, where the others always made a place for her. She wrapped her shawl more tightly around Raina to shield her from the draft coming from the window. Tonight she didn't feel like joining in the conversation that ebbed and swelled around the fire.

Tasha looked at the familiar faces. Few of them were prisoners, as she and Raina were, kept here against their will. They were there because there was simply no place else to go. In the economic chaos that followed Comnor's ascension to the throne, many small businessmen and owners of family farms had lost all they had. Some became beggars, others found a sort of refuge in farm compounds like this one. The labor was unrelenting, privacy and personal time were hard to come by, but there was food to eat, and shelter from the storms.

She looked again at the old man. He was not a beggar; he did not have the beaten look of one who has seen his dreams crumble. Who was he? A wanderer, yes. A hunter. But somehow she felt there was something more. What was he hiding?

The old man made no move from his corner. He was braiding something. When he finished, he quietly turned his chair so that he was by her side.

"I have a gift," he said simply. "For you and the child."

She felt the warmth of his hand as he pressed a small bundle into her palm. She slipped her hands under the edge of the shawl and unwrapped the braided laces.

A blast of cold air hit her face as the old man left the eating room to go to the men's quarters. Tasha hugged Raina closer to her on her lap to stop herself from shivering. But this time the shivering was not from the cold. She did not need to look to know what the old man had given her. It was a necklace, a braided chain of rawhide fastened to a small wooden dove, its wings outstretched in a flight to freedom. She and Raina had not been forgotten.

II

$\mathcal{J}$T WAS STILL DARK WHEN TASHA STUMBLED FROM BED, summoned by the loud clang of the wake-up bell. Long ago she had learned to bundle her clothes and hold them next to her and the child as they slept. It was easier to dress if the rough garments were not stiff with cold. She wrapped a quilt around the still sleeping Raina and carried her down to the eating room. Even children were not allowed the luxury of sleeping late in this place. But Tasha could give her a few minutes more by not waking her until after the morning "history" class.

The old man was lounging by the doorway as she came down the stairs. He had not yet taken his usual place in the corner. Even wanderers had to attend the morning lecture. The labor he was exempt from, but these classes included everyone. As Tasha entered the room he brushed past her on his way to his seat and dropped a small bottle into her apron pocket.

"I'm so sorry," he whispered, "to see your hair turning so white."

She sat in her accustomed place and shifted the sleeping child so that her hand was free. Reaching into her pocket she fingered the bottle. There was a drop of liquid on the outside. Withdrawing her hand, she sniffed her finger. Bleach. The kind the girls used to use to lighten their hair in the old days. It was not strong and would take many applications to make a difference in her dark locks. There would not be enough, not unless . . .

Her hand strayed to the heavy coil of braid on her head. It was the one thing she had left from her old life. It was always with her. A reminder of the happy days with her family.

"But if we are to leave," she thought, "my hair will give us away. Everyone knows of my hair . . ."

It was true. She was known by her hair. She wore her braid coiled like the crown her father had refused for them both. It helped to identify her, even in this place. Those who had loved her father and who looked for the return of Marko and his band had moved over and given her what they could—the seat closest to the fire, soup served from the bottom of the pot where any stray vegetables had settled, help with carrying the large bundles of grain or seed when it would not be noticed.

The educator droned on, pausing now and then to ask a question. Members of the little group answered by rote, their replies as wooden and meaningless as the lecture.

Once more Tasha fingered the bottle in her pocket. To be effective, she would have to cut her hair and comb in the liquid a little every day. She still had a small packet of hairpins that had belonged to her grandmother. They were long and carved from bone. Somehow the guards had missed them when her belongings were searched. Perhaps she could cut off the braid and then use the pins to fasten it back on. It would be less noticeable and the disguise would be more effective if others did not suspect what she was doing.

Tasha's mind was reeling. She didn't even know the name of the Old Man, as everyone called him. His white hair made him look old, and he had never corrected anyone when they started calling him "Old Man." Now Tasha looked up and studied him carefully.

Far from old, his frame was strong and athletic. His hair was white, but it was thick and full, and his face was clean-shaven. But it was his hands that drew her attention. Though they seemed to be resting quietly on his knees, she saw the knuckles whiten even as his jaw tensed with controlled anger at the words spewing from the teacher's mouth. And he was a hunter. Since his arrival there had been the meat for the evening meal. And the wolves no longer howled around the compound at night. It was after the Old Man had arrived that they were silenced.

He shifted his gaze and caught her looking at him. He raised one eyebrow in a question. *Are you willing to come?*

he seemed to say. Tasha raised her hand to the wooden dove, hidden under her dress. She gave a brief nod, *Yes.* She held Raina closer, looked at her sleeping face, and then glanced up again. Once more she nodded. *Yes, we are ready to go.*

The sound of a trumpet interrupted Tasha's thoughts. She stiffened, knowing what was coming. The teacher cut his lesson short and several of the workers hurried from the room. It was better to miss breakfast than to stand around playing court to Comnor. The Old Man was the first to leave, slipping out by way of the kitchen. Through the open door, Tasha saw him speak briefly to the cook, then motion to the kitchen boy to go with him.

Raina had not yet awakened. Tasha held her close, steeling herself and gaining strength from the child. It would do no good for her to leave. She would only be called back.

Comnor entered with a flourish. A dusting of spring snow glittered on his woolen cloak. Tasha sat looking into the fire, her back straight.

"My lord, welcome." It was the old serving woman, simpering and bowing, with a steaming cup of frothy chocolate.

Comnor took the cup and tasted it. "Delicious. Perfect after a brisk ride!"

He set the cup back on the tray and dismissed the old woman with a wave of his hand. From the corner of her eye, Tasha saw him turn back to the others, gathered about the door. She heard the scuffle of feet as the others cleared the room. An aid vanished into the kitchen, shutting the door after him.

Comnor straddled a chair and sat facing her. "Have you reconsidered my proposal, Tasha? Are you ready to come with me?"

His voice flowed smoothly as he laid a saddlebag at her feet. "I brought you a gift."

He opened the bag and pulled out a dress, spreading its softness across her lap.

Tasha could feel its silky smoothness. For an instant she longed to gather it in her arms, hold it against her cheek. Then Raina stirred.

"No, Com." She turned and looked him in the eyes. "The answer is still no. Give your gifts where they will be appreciated. If you want to give me a gift, sell this and buy a dozen warm dresses for the other women here. Some have little more than rags. If you are truly a king, then show it by serving your people."

Comnor stood, kicking the chair aside, his eyes suddenly hard. "I *am* the king, Tasha. Everyone in the kingdom bows at my feet." He shook his fist in front of her face. "*I* am the king."

"Enjoy it while you can, Com." Tasha's eyes were steady on his face. "The republic is not dead. Marko and the others will return, and then we'll see how many will still bow at your feet."

"Marko!" he spat on the fire. "Marko's ragtag followers have that much chance against my armies." He leaned his face into hers, "You don't even know if Marko is still alive. Two years is a long time. Many were wounded in the battle that sent them running across the river. If you want to go back to your old home, Tasha, it will be as my queen."

Unblinking, Tasha stared at him. "Marko is alive, Com, and I would rather die here than live one minute as your wife."

Com turned and spoke through clenched teeth. "Your chances are numbered, Tasha. I won't keep asking forever." He glanced at Raina, now awake and staring at him in fear. His voice softened. "Think of the child. Surely you don't want her to grow up here? Bring her with you. Think of what you can do as queen."

Gathering Raina more tightly in her arms, Tasha stood, spilling the dress to the floor. "My father abdicated the throne, Com, or don't you remember? This kingdom of yours is a sham. Marko is president of the new republic, and when he returns, the people who elected him will rise up against you."

She turned away, but Com reached out and took her by the shoulders. "Marko was a traitor who deceived you and your father. When your father died, I knew the best way to honor his memory would be to bring back the old rule—to put things back the way they were before Marko interfered."

Tasha trembled as she struggled to control her anger. Com would never understand. Wrenching herself from his grasp, she turned toward the door. Carefully she set Raina on the floor, took her hand, and walked from the room, the wooden dove warm under the coarse wool of her dress.

III

OMNOR WAS GONE LONG BEFORE TASHA RETURNED from her work in the fields. The Old Man was sitting on a stump near the side of the barn, dressing out a rabbit. As she approached he stood and carried the offal to the dogs chained to the enclosure gate. Only the guards could approach the dogs without raising a cacophony of barking, but this was obviously not the first time the Old Man had supplemented their meager diet. They stood silent, wagging their tails as he walked among them. He let them smell his clothing while he divided the food so that each received an equal share.

Tasha waited by the stump until he returned for the carcass.

"It must take a very sharp knife to skin an animal so well and to keep oneself so clean-shaven," she said.

"Wanderers carry what they will," he replied. "And even

those who run a place such as this know a hunter has need of a knife."

The last of the workers were filing through the gate. Tasha turned quickly to join them. The Old Man picked up the rabbit and headed for the kitchen. She saw him pause at the kitchen door to speak to the boy who tended the stoves. The Old Man ruffled the boy's hair and then handed him the rabbit. He took it with a grin and ran inside.

After picking up Raina from the weaving rooms, she hurried her over to the outside pump. The water from the pump was cold for washing, but no one else was there. The others preferred the relative luxury of warmer water from the indoor faucets.

Tasha pulled a coarse cloth from her pocket, wet it, and wiped the grime from Raina's face and hands.

"Raina," she whispered, "if no one is standing behind us from here to the barn, nod your head. If someone approaches us say out loud, 'That hurts.'"

Her eyes wide, the little girl carefully scanned the area behind Tasha and then quickly nodded.

"Do you know who the man is that everyone calls the Old Man?"

There was another nod.

"Marko has sent him. He will take us to him. I don't know yet when we will leave, but we must be ready. *You must say nothing.* Do you understand?"

The little girl started to cry out with excitement, but Tasha quickly put the cloth on Raina's lips and shook her head. "Say nothing or we may never be able to leave. You must understand this."

"I understand," Raina whispered.

Tasha continued to scrub the little girl's hands and face and smooth back her hair. "Please try not to ask questions. I will tell you all that I can as soon as I know."

"Ouch, Tasha, that hurts," Raina said out loud.

Tasha straightened herself and turned to see Olaf, the burly outside guard coming around the side of the barn.

"Trying to scrub off the little one's skin?" he asked. "And with cold water, too. I would think only hot water would be good enough for the little sister of Marko the great."

Tasha shook her skirts to straighten them and took Raina's hand. "It is less crowded out here. And cold water is good for the complexion." She managed a smile. "Don't you agree?"

Taken aback by her unexpected friendliness he stood in confusion. "Yes, yes, of course." He stumbled over the words. "But I am on my way to ring the evening bell. You must be inside."

"Thank you for warning us, Olaf. Come, Raina, it is time for supper." Tasha turned and, still holding tightly to Raina's hand, walked quickly into the dining hall.

They slipped inside and found their places before the clang of the bell brought the others to their seats. There was still a half hour of evening lecture to endure before the meal would be served. Plenty of time for the cook to add the Old Man's rabbit to whatever they were eating.

It seemed as if the teacher droned on longer than usual. He had summed up his speech, but still he rambled on. Tasha looked up in time to see him glance toward the kitchen doorway. The boy who worked in the kitchen gave a nod and the lecture came to a quick end.

"So," thought Tasha with a smile, "he wanted the rabbit to be ready as well."

It was only natural. Everyone was fed the same. Even the few babies, once they were weaned, were given whatever was on the adult menu, together with a fork so their mothers could mash up the food for their toothless gums.

After the meal, Tasha again placed her chair at the end of the row. On the other side of the room, Josie, a young girl with unruly auburn hair and blue eyes, started to tell a story, poking fun at one of the several young men who always seemed to surround her, even during work. As the tale grew more animated, she rocked back on her chair, tipping it over. The others rushed to help her up. The Old Man stood also in the confusion, moved to Tasha's side, and slipped a small folded knife into her hand. The group parted as he strode over and gave Josie his hand, pulling her to her feet.

"Wonderful story," he said, straightening her chair. "Too bad the evening does not allow for more." Then he turned and quickly left the room.

Usually Tasha had no trouble falling asleep after the long workday, but this night she willed herself to only doze off. The full moon was high in the sky when she jerked fully awake and quietly slid from bed. The small round window in their tiny room would not open, but it gave a glimpse of the sky and allowed a sliver of moonlight to filter in. Tasha and Raina had been allowed to have this bedroom to themselves, partly because Raina was so young and partly because the housekeeper was sympathetic to Tasha. The room was smaller than any one of Tasha's closets in her old home, but she was grateful for this small measure of privacy.

Moving to the door, she paused to listen. The house was still. Only the snores of the old woman who served tables could be heard. Tonight Tasha had not undressed, as she usually did. She had lain quietly in bed, clutching the small knife, her hand in her pocket.

Now, gathering her shawl around her for warmth, Tasha sat on the floor. It would not do for Olaf or one of the other outside guards to see a shadow moving in her room. Slowly she undid the braid that kept her hair tightly bound. She sat there for a long time combing it, letting its softness flow around her shoulders and down her back.

For a few minutes she forgot the cold, the hard floor, and the tiny room. Once again she was sitting in the sunshine beside the lake, combing her hair dry after her swim. Marko was coming up the road with his baby sister balanced on his hip, his short blond curls stuck to his head from the heat and dust. His pale skin and sunken cheeks showed that he was another victim of the fever outbreak in the southern cities. She guessed, rightly as she learned later, that the disease had claimed his parents, as it would claim her own mother in another year.

"Do you know where a clever boy can find work?"

"Talk to Samuel up at the workshop. He is always looking for those who can learn quickly," she said.

Marko had just stood there, watching her comb her hair. Only when she paused to look at him sharply had he turned and walked briskly toward the house with its cluster of outbuildings.

A dog barked, abruptly ending her reverie, and Tasha was back in the little room, with the hard floor, the little window, and Raina sleeping peacefully on the narrow bed. She stopped combing, put her arms over her bowed head, covered her face with her heavy hair, and wept.

A cloud moved to block the stream of moonlight. Tasha sat up straight, stretched, and quickly dried her tears. All day she had been thinking of this moment. She could not cut it too short, or it would not blend in with the false braid. Gathering her locks together she tied them tightly with a string just above her shoulders. Then, for the last time she made her braid, over and under, under and over, tight and neat. Another string firmly bound the end. The knife was razor sharp. In an instant it was done, and she held the thick rope of hair in her hands.

Then, taking the little bottle the Old Man had given her, she poured out some of the liquid and combed it into her short hair. It would take several applications, but gradually her hair would turn from black to gray.

For the next hour she practiced coiling the braid, fastening it with the hairpins, blending it with the rest. "If only I had a mirror," she thought. But she could go only by feel. Finally, satisfied, she slid back into bed, gradually relaxing under the warmth of the quilt. She had put her feet on the path that would take them away from this place. She fell asleep, one arm around the sleeping child, her other hand holding the little wooden dove.

IV

THE NEXT MORNING, TASHA WOKE RAINA BEFORE going down to breakfast instead of letting her sleep, as she usually did. She held the little girl's hand as they walked down the stairs. The Old Man was leaning casually against the wall near the doorway, watching as the others filed into the dining room. Tasha stopped, one hand in her pocket.

"Old Man, you have been here for several weeks and I do not know your name," she said quietly.

"Some call me Ari," he answered, "but for here, 'the Old Man' is good enough."

She took her hand from her pocket and held it out to him, "I give you our thanks for the meat and the help you have given us."

He enveloped her small hand in his. "It is a pleasure for a wanderer to find a refuge, even for a little while."

Ari took the knife she had passed him and slid it into his

pocket. Then he moved quickly to speak to Josie, the girl who had told such a good story the night before. As Tasha turned to take her seat she saw Olaf, standing in the shadow of the kitchen doorway, his small sharp eyes watching them. Had he seen her pass the knife?

All day as she worked in the fields, Tasha held her head carefully, afraid that a sudden movement would dislodge the heavy braid and cause it to fall. The hairpins held, but by evening her neck was stiff and sore.

As they entered the compound Ari was again sitting on the stump. The boy from the kitchen was there, too. Tasha was first in line as they entered the gate, and she saw the boy in earnest conversation with Ari. Looking up, the boy quickly turned his back to the incoming workers. Ari gave him a short reply and then handed him the squirrel he had been dressing out. The boy turned and ran to the kitchen.

The spring air was mild, but Tasha could smell the scent of an approaching storm as she again led Raina to the outside pump to wash up. After feeding the dogs, Ari strode over to the pump, squatting down to wash his hands and his knife.

"Olaf is suspicious," he said. "He saw you pass me the knife this morning. He wasn't sure what it was, but he reported it anyway. I had hoped for more time, but I'm afraid we will have to leave tonight."

"Tonight?" Tasha stopped washing Raina's face, the cloth suspended in her hand. She looked up at the clouds scudding across the sky.

Ari stood. "The storm will help us. The night will be dark. Come to the stump beside the barn as soon as the house is silent." He shook the water from his knife and wiped it on his pant leg. "Dress warmly. I have food, but bring blankets if you can."

Folding the knife, he placed it in his pocket and walked toward the kitchen. "Boy!" he called. "Come and help. I saw some fresh greens today." The kitchen boy ran outside to join him.

Tasha did not hear more of their conversation. She straightened up, took Raina's hand, and hurried toward the dining hall. At the doorway she paused to compose herself.

"Tasha," Raina said softly, "are you afraid?"

Tasha looked into the trusting eyes of the child. Taking a deep breath she glanced over to where Ari was talking and laughing with the boy as they gathered dandelion leaves. "No, Raina," she said, "I'm not afraid. Ari will help us and God will protect us." She gave the small hand a gentle squeeze. "There is no need to fear."

Together they walked inside.

The evening meal proceeded as every evening meal had in the two years since they had been forced to come to this place. There was the usual lecture, the bowls of soup, coarse bread, and cold water. The only difference was the small cup beside Raina's plate. After Ari drove off the wolves, a few skinny cows were allowed on pickets outside the walls to graze on the new spring grass. One of the cows had calved three weeks ago, and tonight there was a bit of milk for the few children.

Tonight Tasha resumed her place in the center of the semicircle around the fire after supper. She joined in the conversation, speaking to each person in turn, etching their names and faces into her memory. They had shared so much, and though there was little enough that each one had, so many of them had given what they could to make life a little easier for her and for Raina. Now she and Raina were leaving, and she couldn't even tell them "thank you." They would all be questioned, and it would go easier on them if they honestly knew nothing of what was happening.

As usual, it was Ari who was the first to leave. Tonight he finished carving a wooden spoon for one of the women who worked in the kitchen. He gave it to her as he left, and Tasha saw her pleased expression as she examined its sturdy smoothness. Tasha left soon after, carrying Raina, who had fallen asleep on her lap, lulled by the hum of voices and the warmth of the fire.

Back in her little room, Tasha stripped the bedding from the bed, wrapped the sleeping Raina in her shawl, and laid her on the mattress. Then she went to work quickly and quietly. She had no way to cover the little window and she did not have much time before even the pale light from her candle stub would cause suspicion. Spreading a sheet on the floor, she folded it over their extra clothing, fashioning a rude backpack. Cutting through the selvage with her teeth, she tore strips from another sheet. The winter quilt would be too bulky and heavy to carry, but she could take the lighter quilt and the two wool blankets they had been given. One blanket she rolled tightly, tying it with strips from the sheet. Other strips made crude straps. Raina would have to carry at least part of the load. The other blanket and the quilt were folded together, then rolled and fastened onto the top of her pack.

She removed her long braid. It would only be in the way now. As she ran her fingers through her hair she thought of the small bottle of bleach. There was no need now to be sparing in its application. The faster her hair whitened, the better. Removing the bottle from her pocket, she worked the liquid into her hair. Raina stirred as the smell filled the little room. Tasha hoped the odor would not escape into the hall. While the bleach worked she continued to sort their few belongings. Then filling her wash basin with water from a pitcher, she quickly washed her hair.

She dropped the empty bottle back into her pocket and covered her damp hair with a scarf, tying it back, off her face. The carved bone hairpins she tied together and tucked into a deep pocket. Perhaps they would not survive the trip, but they had been with her this long. She would at least try to take them with her.

It bothered her that her pack was light colored. It was too visible. She would need to cover it with her dark shawl.

Finally there was nothing more to do but to wait and to pray. She blew out the candle and sat on the floor under the little window. She was afraid she would sleep too deeply if she lay on the mattress. Outside, the wind lashed the trees. There was no moonlight coming into the room tonight. It wouldn't be long before the rain would come, great splashing drops punctuated by thunder and lightning. She leaned against the wall in a doze.

She had always hated nights like this. She would awaken to the fury of the storm and lie trembling in her bed. When she could stand it no longer she used to call out and her mother or father would come to her room and hold her hand until she fell asleep.

Once she mentioned her fears to Marko. "A storm is nothing to fear," he said. "If we have done our work well, then God will protect us."

And Marko had always done his work well. If he had been given charge of the barn, then the animals would be inside, there would be clean water in the inside trough and fresh hay in the mangers. If he had been working in the shop, the fire would be out, the coals carried outside, the door barred, and the shutters secure against the storm.

Before she met Marko, Tasha never bothered herself with such things. She would often start a project and never finish, leaving the mess for one of the maids to clean up. Then, one evening, before they had even spoken many words to each other, she had passed the kitchen and seen him helping the scullery maid clean up a mess she had left after making pastry. She intended for the pastry to impress Marko. She had stood in the shadow of the hall, watching him carefully clean the table, her cheeks burning with shame. She was only glad that she had not had a chance to give him the pastry. The maid was loyal. She had never revealed who made the mess, and Marko had never mentioned it. But never again did Tasha leave her work for someone else to do.

A distant rumble of thunder brought Tasha awake with a start. Except for the snoring of the old serving woman, the house was silent. It was time to go.

V

"Raina, raina," tasha whispered, gently shaking the child. "Raina, it's time to go."

The little girl sat up and sleepily rubbed her eyes. "Are we going to Marko now?" she asked.

"Yes," Tasha replied. "It will take many days, but we are going to Marko. Here, you must carry this blanket."

Moving in the dark, Tasha helped Raina down from the bed and then smoothed the big winter quilt over the mattress. She secured the small bundle on Raina's back, then shouldered her own pack, wrapping and tying it with her shawl. When Marko had first arrived, asking for work, he had been assigned to help Old Samuel in the stables. Tasha had often been assigned to help care for Raina. She loved to play with her and often carried her like that, wrapped and tied in her shawl on her back. It was easier than trying to keep her entertained. The baby had loved it, peeking over Tasha's shoulder, watching everything that went on, close and secure next to Tasha.

Before she closed the door after them, Tasha turned for one last look. The lamplight from the hall made things in the room dimly visible. It was then that she saw the braid, lying on the floor under the little window. Stepping quickly back inside, she picked it up and stuffed it into her dress. If they found the braid, even this small disguise would be useless. One more glance told her there was nothing else left to take. She put a small piece of paper in the door latch to wedge it shut, then pulled the door closed. Tasha took Raina by the hand, and they made their way down the stairs and out into the approaching storm.

As they stepped outside, the wind whipped the clouds away from the moon, bathing the yard in white light. Tasha pulled Raina to her and shrank back into the shadow of the building. A minute later the clouds once again covered the moon and only the darker shape of the walls and the barn could be distinguished.

They ran toward the side of the barn. Ari was there, waiting in the shadows.

"Come," he said, taking her by the elbow. "We must try to reach the river before the rain begins."

As they approached the gate, the dogs crowded around them. Tasha froze in fear, clutching Raina to her side. But instead of barking, the dogs merely sniffed at them, recognizing Ari's scent. He reached into his jacket and pulled out a packet of bones, saved from the stew they had eaten at supper. The dogs crowded around, each vying for a share. Ari tossed the bones away in a wide arc, then taking Tasha's arm once more, led them through a small door beside the main gate.

"It is always good to have friends," Ari whispered, "even if they are dogs."

The wind whipped at them as Ari led the way down the road toward a branch of the Reed River. After they had walked nearly a mile, he veered off the path into the trees. A small creek gurgled along about a quarter of a mile into the woods.

"Wait here," Ari said, plunging in, and wading downstream. After going only a short way, he pulled out another packet of bones and scattered them on the bank, leaving the wrapping paper loosely hidden under a stone, covered with a few leaves. Then, turning around, he returned the way he had come, exiting the stream on the grass where he had entered it.

"Now we will go back to the road and follow it to the compound," he said. "This is an old trick and will put them off for only a little while, but that may be all we need."

Raina started to tire before they reached the compound. Ari hoisted her on his back and carried her piggyback. Now they could travel more quickly. At the compound gate, Ari turned and started to follow the well-worn path toward the fields. Because everyone in the compound had traveled that pathway, it would be hard for the dogs to distinguish their scents on that trail. The fields were newly plowed, but there were pathways between some of the rows, made by the planters the day before. Once again, their scent would be mingled with that of others, and with the rain would hopefully not attract the dogs.

The fields were surrounded by woods but these were woods where Ari hunted every day. "I've been taking others from the compound hunting with me the last two weeks," he explained. "I wanted to make sure that several others also traveled each of the trails I cleared through the underbrush."

Only when they had traveled for some time in the woods did Ari veer onto a nearly hidden animal trail. There was a snare on the trail and now it held a rabbit. Carefully, Ari stepped over the animal, then turned and taking Tasha by the waist, lifted her over it as well.

"The animals of the forest have helped us a great deal," Ari said. "This rabbit will help to stop the dogs. And if the guards are quick enough, it may enrich the stew this evening. Maybe even Olaf will stop searching for us and look instead for the other snares in the other part of the forest."

The animal trail was harder to follow. Branches and brambles tore at Tasha's skirts. Too often she had to stop and pull herself loose. Once the wind whipped a branch down in front of her face. Instinctively she ducked as a twig snatched at the scarf on her head, nearly pulling it off.

Finally Ari stepped into a clearing at the edge of the

main channel of the Reed River and lowered Raina to the ground. Then he turned to Tasha.

"Do you have something of yours that you can give up?" he asked.

Tasha started to shake her head, then thought of the braid tucked inside her dress. She drew it out. "There is this," she said. "I didn't know what to do with it."

"Excellent!" Ari said, taking it from her. "This may serve us well."

From the bushes near the river he pulled a crudely made raft. Each log was marked with a deep blaze. Taking some torn pieces of cloth from inside his shirt, he wedged some into cracks in the logs. Then he did the same with several strands of the long hair, twisting them in and around the bark. The rest of the braid he separated and scattered with the remaining rags into the raging water. "The cloth and the hair should carry our scents down the river."

He shoved the raft into the middle of the stream, gouging the soil of the bank.

"With a raft, one can go only downstream," Ari explained. "This will break up before reaching the sea. A small ship will leave the port of Bismire as soon as the debris is found and identified, but it will be seen flying a black flag. How terrible to have to take a message to Marko and the others that his sister and the princess Tasha were lost on a raft on the river during the spring floods."

Tasha looked up in alarm. "Will they reach Marko with

such a message? If he thinks something has happened to Raina, he will be inconsolable. We must find some way to stop them."

"They will reach Marko, and give him that message," Ari said, and Tasha could tell from his voice that he was smiling. "But knowing the raft has broken up will only tell him that we escaped safely. It is one of the many signals we have arranged. That Marko always does a job most thoroughly."

"Yes," Tasha murmured, thinking back to her earlier reflections in the little room, "yes, Marko always does a thorough job."

The thunder rumbled closer.

"Come," Ari said with urgency. "We must try to reach shelter before the storm breaks."

Without another word he hoisted Raina onto his back. "Do you know how to swim?" he asked Tasha above the howl of the wind.

"Yes, I have swum since I was a child the age of Raina."

"Good," he said, "because the water is deep in the middle and the current is strong from the first of the spring rains." He handed her a long leather strap with a loop on each end. "Hook this around my belt and fasten the other loop around your left arm. It will help to keep us together."

"Now, little one," he said to Raina, "hold on tight and don't let go."

Ari picked up a short length of log and handed it to

Tasha. "Use this to help you stay afloat." He picked up another one for himself and plunged into the river.

Tasha gasped as she stepped into the icy water. The current swirled around her, nearly knocking her off her feet. She twisted the strap more tightly around her wrist and walked forward. Long before they reached the middle, it seemed, she could no longer keep her footing on the bottom. She kicked her feet and pushed the log ahead of her. Her skirts and the pack on her back kept trying to drag her down. A sudden rush of water caught the log and wrenched it from her grasp. Calling on reserves she did not know she had, she swam, keeping her eyes always on the dark shape of Ari ahead of her. Finally, she saw him stand. Reaching down with her feet, she felt the sandy bottom of the riverbed. Stumbling forward, her legs and feet numb with cold, she grasped the strap with both hands and allowed Ari to pull her the rest of the way.

Her wrist was bleeding where the strap had cut into it and her hand was numb. She unwound the leather. The rush of blood to her cold hand nearly made her sob with pain. She bit her lip until she could taste blood to keep from crying out. But already Ari was striding forward, his head bowed in fatigue, his steps urgent.

She groped after him, making her way by the flashes of lightning. She half wished that they were still bound together by the leather strap. That would be better than being lost in these woods. Once she did lose him, and stopped, not knowing which way to go. There was a streak of lightning, followed by a clap of thunder.

"Tasha!" It was Raina's voice, there, ahead, and to the right. "Tasha! Where are you?"

Tasha pushed her way through the undergrowth to find Ari waiting, resting for a minute on a fallen log, Raina clinging to his arm.

"Hurry," he said. "It's not far now."

The storm broke as they started up the slope of a hill. The rain fell in sheets, making it impossible for her to see.

"Ari!" she screamed. "Give me the strap. I can't see."

He stopped and once more she fastened the strap around her wrist, now throbbing and beginning to swell. She reached out for the bushes with her right hand, using them to pull her upward, even as the wind tossed them at her and tried to push her back.

On an outcrop of rock near the top of the hill, Ari paused. He inched sideways along the narrow ledge, struggling to balance himself. Instinctively, Raina flattened herself against his back, holding on with her legs and arms. Tasha let the leather strap slip from her wrist. They could not risk everyone's falling. For a moment she stood in the rain, hugging the rock as the lightning flashed and the thunder rolled, echoing through the woods and hills. She looked over toward Ari and saw him beckon to her, then suddenly, with the next flash of lightning, he was gone.

A crash of thunder drove her to her knees. The raindrops on her cheeks felt warm and as they ran salty into her mouth, she knew they were tears.

Then she heard Ari calling her name, and just as suddenly as he had vanished, he was there again, standing on the ledge, beckoning to her.

"Tasha, here. Try to catch the rope."

With the next lightning flash, she saw a rope come snaking through the air toward her. As the light faded, she reached out into the dark night and grabbed the end. Tying it around her waist, she held it with one hand and followed the wall of the cliff with the other. Once she slipped as the rock beneath her feet crumbled with the rain and the weight of her body. She reached out blindly toward the cliff and her hand closed around the slender trunk of a piñon pine, growing out of a crack in the rock. Then the ledge widened, and she felt the warmth of Ari's hand as he grasped her wrist and pulled her the last few feet.

Ari bent down and pushed aside a small bush. It was the entrance to a cave. Raina was waiting inside. The air was cold but it was dry. Tasha sank down on the sandy floor and took the child in her arms.

It seemed she had only had time to catch her breath when Ari spoke.

"I'm sorry, but we cannot stay here." There was the sound of flint on steel, and the flash of a spark, and then a torch flared to life.

Wearily Tasha rose to her feet and took Raina's hand.

"Stand over there on that shelf of rock." Ari motioned with his hand.

Tasha stood and walked to the low outcropping of rock

and stepped up onto it. Taking a small brushy limb from a corner, Ari smoothed out the sand that had blown into the cave entrance, erasing the evidence of their passing. Then, stepping carefully onto the rock, he led the way into the interior of the cave.

At first Tasha tried to remember the way they were traveling, but soon she gave up and focused all her will on just moving forward, keeping the light in view. The passages twisted and turned, some of them so low that even Raina had to stoop to avoid hitting her head. Then, all at once, Tasha felt the cave open up. They were in another room, larger than the one at the entrance. In the distance she could hear the murmur of an underground stream. The air was cold and damp. Her clothes, wet from the river and from the rain, seemed to drag her down.

"Ari," she managed a whisper that echoed back to her. "I don't know how much longer I can go on."

Ari moved back and took her hand. "You don't have to go any farther. This is the place I have prepared for us to rest for a while."

He walked over to where an underground stream had once washed out a small cove, leaving a sandy floor before moving on to another channel. Dipping the torch toward the floor he lit a fire lay. Then he turned and handed the torch to Tasha.

"If you go forward just a little way, you will find another small cove. Inside are dry clothes for you and the child. Leave your blankets. I will hang them to dry beside the fire."

Gratefully Tasha slipped off the heavy pack and took the torch. In the little room Ari had left trousers and shirts for both of them. He had even been able to secure underclothing, wrapped neatly in a small bundle. Tasha shed the heavy wet skirts with a sigh of relief. The woolen trousers and cotton shirts were rough, but they were warm. She hung the wet clothing over the rocks to dry as best they could, then, taking Raina's hand, walked back to the fire.

Already Ari had some soup warmed and ready for them to drink. The hot liquid helped disperse the chill, and gradually Tasha began to relax in the warmth of the fire. Little Raina had managed only a couple of swallows before she set her soup bowl down, put her head on Tasha's lap, and fell asleep.

Ari had laid out some furs on the floor of the cove. Gently he lifted the child onto a furry robe and covered her with a dry blanket.

"We will be safe here," Ari said. "Use that robe beside Raina for your bed. I will sleep on the other side of the fire."

Tasha snuggled gratefully into the soft warmth of the furs. Ari produced another blanket and she pulled it around her shoulders.

Tasha never knew how long she had slept, but the fire was only glowing coals when she awoke. For a minute she didn't know where she was. She turned over on her side and every muscle in her body seemed to scream with pain. She felt the soft fur next to her face and remembered their escape, the long tramp through the woods in the wind, the river crossing, the cliff in the dark, the rain, and then the welcome safety of the cave.

Ari had said they were safe here, yet something had awakened her. What was it? Straining her eyes against the blackness she looked back toward the tunnel entrance. There was a brief flash of light, as if someone was striking a match and then quickly blowing it out. But in its brief flash Tasha knew what she had seen. Someone had followed them into the cave.

VI

WITH THE DIM LIGHT FROM THE COALS TASHA could make out the form of Ari sleeping on the other side of the fire. Trying to stay out of the reflection from the fire, Tasha edged herself around until she could nudge him with her foot. Though he did not move, Tasha felt his body stiffen and knew that he had come instantly awake. As carefully as she could, she withdrew into the blackness, taking Raina in her arms.

There was the scrape of a shoe on a pebble. Tasha saw the shadow of Ari's arm reach out and then back toward the glowing coals. Suddenly there was a burst of light as the torch in Ari's hand caught fire. Tasha shrank back to the far wall of the cove, shielding her eyes from the light. In one fluid motion, Ari stood, passed the torch to his left hand, and drew a long hunting knife from his belt with the other. He stepped forward, the light from the torch searching the darkness for the intruder.

"Ari!" It was the voice of a youth, not yet a man.

Ari stepped toward the sound. The light revealed the boy from the kitchen, trembling with cold.

"So . . ." Ari's voice was gruff. "You decided to leave. You must get out of those wet clothes. Here." Ari threw him a blanket. "You'll have to use this until your clothes are dry."

The boy moved briefly away from the light. Ari took some wood and dumped it on the coals. There was still some soup left. He scraped some coals from the blaze and made a bed for the pot.

It didn't take long for the boy to remove his ragged clothing. He approached the fire warily, wanting the warmth, yet embarrassed to be wearing only a blanket.

Filling his own bowl with stew for the boy, Ari gave it to him and then stood. "I must see that the tracks are gone from the entrance," he said, and taking the torch, disappeared down the tunnel.

The boy was too hungry and cold to talk. Tasha stayed back in the shadows, still holding the sleeping Raina. Once the boy glanced her way and then turned hungrily back to his soup. She could see his face gradually start to relax as his bowl emptied and the warmth of the fire filled the little cove. Once, then twice, his head nodded, then the bowl clattered from his fingers, and he rolled up in the blanket and slept.

Tasha, too, returned to her bed of furs and was soon asleep. She was only dimly aware of Ari's return and the "s-s-s-t" of the torch as Ari extinguished it in the stream at the back of the cavern before returning to his own bed on the other side of the fire. Once more the flames died down and the cave was plunged into darkness.

It was hunger and the bright light of the fire Ari was building up that finally awakened both Tasha and Raina. The unmoving form of the boy still lay curled in the spot where he had drifted off to sleep. Tasha noticed that Ari had covered him with another blanket, *probably his own,* she thought.

When the coals were just right, Ari put a flat rock on them to heat. Then he mixed some cornmeal and water and began to bake some little cakes. Soon the smell of corn cakes mingled with the aroma of hot stew.

Eagerly little Raina held out her bowl. Tasha felt her own stomach growl in anticipation. For a while they ate in silence. Then, when the hunger was not so sharp, Tasha spoke in a low voice.

"The kitchen boy. How did he find us?"

"I knew he wanted to come," Ari said. "For the last three weeks I had permission to take him hunting with me a few hours at a time. He gathered wood, so they did not object. When I knew he could be trusted, I gave him directions to the cave. He was supposed to leave several days after we did, but perhaps, with the storm, it is better this way. They will not want to track even four people for very long in such a rain."

"Is it still raining, then?" Tasha asked.

"Yes, still very hard. And now snow and sleet are mixed

with it. It is good we left when we did. The ground was still firm and we left few tracks. I hope they will see the gouge on the riverbank and think we have gone down the river. But now we must stay here for a while. We cannot risk going out and being followed."

"Is it night?" Raina asked, looking around at the blackness.

"No, little one," Ari answered. "Remember, when we entered the cave last night? No light can come down here. We are like little mice, safe and sound in a burrow under the ground."

Raina giggled at the thought, then snuggled back down into her bed of furs and blankets and closed her eyes.

Ari rose and moved the boy's clothes closer to the fire to finish drying.

"Do you think," he said as he eyed the ragged pants and torn shirt, "do you think you could take some of the cloth from your skirts and make the boy some other clothes?"

"I would need a sharp knife to cut the cloth and a needle and thread," Tasha answered. "But yes, I know how to sew. Father said it was important to know how to do whatever needed to be done in a home. My governess made me sit and sew for hours. I hated it."

She looked up at Ari and smiled sadly. "I thought he didn't know what he was talking about. His counsel was wiser than I think even he knew."

Ari stood and walked to a large pack propped up against the wall. He reached in, pulled out a small bundle, and tossed it to Tasha. "Here are needles and thread. The thread is not plentiful. Use it wisely. The knife you will find behind you, near the wall. It is for you to keep. If something happens to me, you will need it to survive."

Tasha fingered the small bundle. "Ari, why did it take so long for you to come? Why didn't Marko send for us sooner?"

"It took a while before we knew where you were. Com has more than one compound built for the poor and for his political prisoners. But even after we knew, the council voted to wait before sending someone to get you out."

"But surely Marko"—her words failed her. She swallowed against the lump of anger and hurt in her throat. "Two years... and little Raina..." Tasha turned her head.

She saw the shadow as Ari reached out his hand toward her, but then he drew it back, turned, and busied himself with one of the packs. "It wasn't Marko. He would have followed you the first day. But we couldn't risk it. We needed him. Your time in the compound was hard, but we knew Com would never take your life. And we knew you would protect Raina."

He stepped toward her, turned, and took her gently by the shoulders, his blue eyes dark in the firelight. "Surely, Tasha, you of all people know that this is bigger than any one of us. It isn't just your happiness, Raina's, or Marko's. It is the future of our country that is in the balance—all that your father worked for.

She turned away. Ari dropped his hands. "Tasha, as long

as he had your life in his hands, Com thought he had won. He didn't even follow us across the river when he could have easily destroyed us. But every day people have come to our side. Now we are ready to face him. We could not attack until you were safe. But the White Dove has flown. Com, and every person in the underground, knows that it is only a matter of time now until Marko returns."

He picked up another torch, lit it, and started toward the back of the cavern.

She watched the light as it reflected off the stalactites and stalagmites. Then she saw the shadow of another tunnel as he turned and disappeared into its mouth.

She looked over at the children, asleep in the firelight. Whatever the future, whatever the past, she had work to do now. The kitchen boy needed clothes.

She picked up the knife and felt the razor-sharp blade. What was it that Ari had said? It was important. It had something to do with the knife. *If something happens to me* ...That was it. Her mind started racing. Would something happen to him? She didn't even know for sure where they were. Could she take care of Raina and the boy by herself? Could she find her way alone to the Great North River?

VII

ASHA SHOOK HERSELF. SHE COULD NOT WASTE TIME thinking about "What ifs." The kitchen boy would soon be awake. He would need food and he certainly needed new clothes.

Taking the torch to light her way, Tasha walked over to the other cove where she had left her clothes. Gathering her dress and petticoats which were still damp from the rain and the river, she made her way back to the fire.

The old clothes would provide something of a pattern, but as she remembered, they were too small and fit poorly. She would have to make the new ones much larger. The knife easily cut through the worn thread on the old pants. They had been made the easy way with only three seams. Her dress was better made. It was wool, one of the ones she had taken with her when she and Raina were forced to leave. She herself had helped make the cloth it was cut from, and the homespun was woven tight and even. Still, it had had almost constant use in the past two years, and the threads of the seams were weak.

"Raina," Tasha called softly, trying not to wake the boy. "Light the torch that is near the wall and bring it to me, please. I need you to hold it so I can see to cut the cloth."

Raina did as she was told and from the increased light, Tasha could see a smooth-topped outcropping of rock along the wall, not far off.

Tasha gathered up the cloth. "Come over here, Raina," she said. "This is much better for cutting on. Hold the light in front so that there are fewer shadows."

Laying out the cloth, she cut the pants from the material of her skirt. Then she ripped apart the boy's shirt and cut him another one from her white petticoat.

"Now rub the torch in the sand and put it out," Tasha instructed. "We must not use it more than necessary. I don't know what Ari has been able to gather. The fire will give me enough light for sewing."

Raina watched silently as Tasha carefully stitched the seams of the pants. As she worked, Tasha became aware of the solemn eyes following her every mood. "She has been robbed of her childhood," Tasha thought. "First the death of her parents when she was a baby and then her confinement in that workhouse called a compound." Into her mind sprang pictures of her own childhood, when she had learned to sew. Yes, her father had insisted that she learn and she did not enjoy the task, but the governess who taught her was pleasant and happy and filled the long hours with stories and songs.

Quickly Tasha set the pants aside for a minute and sewed up the sides of the shirt. "Here, Raina," she said, holding it out to her. "This shirt has need of a hem. You can do that. Just roll the edge in your fingers and make tiny stitches like these."

The long days Raina had spent in the weaving rooms at the compound had made her fingers strong and nimble. In only a few minutes her stitches were nearly as neat as Tasha's.

"Do you know what this cave reminds me of, Raina?" Tasha asked.

The little girl shook her head.

"It reminds me of the story of Grandfather Mole, and his grandson, little Bumbler."

With that, Tasha launched into the folktales of her childhood, telling one after another, the darkness of the cave receding before the images of their imaginations.

"There!" Tasha said, as her sewing and another story came to an end at the same time. "Now when the kitchen boy wakes up, he'll have some new clothes to wear."

Raina started to giggle. "Tasha, he *is* awake. He has been listening to the stories forever!"

Tasha turned and saw the kitchen boy drawn up in the shadows, still wrapped in his blanket. She smiled at him and held out the pants. "Here, boy. These are crudely done, but the cloth is heavy and warm. Raina, give him the shirt."

Raina shyly held out the shirt and the boy smiled briefly as he took it from her outstretched hand. Gathering the blanket around him, he hobbled around the outcrop of rock that made up their little room and dressed in the darkness.

"What is your name, boy?" Tasha asked as he returned.

"Just 'boy,'" he said as he fumbled in the jumble of furs and opened packs and finally found a length of rope. He cinched it around his waist to hold up the pants which Tasha had cut too generously, then wrapped himself again in the blanket and sat down close to the small fire.

"But Ari said my true name is 'Gil' and that is what I should be called."

"How would a wanderer such as Ari know your true name?" Tasha asked.

The boy shrugged. "I don't know. When he first came to the compound I used to see him watching me. One day when I was washing, he came up behind me and asked about a mark I have on my back. I wouldn't even know I had it except that once some boys teased me about it when we were swimming. Then I heard him talking to the cook about me. It was right after that he started taking me hunting with him. And then he said my rightful name was Gil, and to always remember it but never tell a royalist."

He bent over and stirred the fire. "I always wanted to have a true name, and Gil is a good solid one. I like to think that perhaps it came from my real parents, that maybe they cared at least enough to name me."

"Of course your parents cared for you," Tasha said. "I feel sure that it was not their choice..."

Tasha stopped speaking as the sound of a falling rock echoed through the chamber. Quickly Gil pulled apart the burning sticks and smothered the sparks with sand. Tasha grabbed Raina's hand and pulled her into the shadows of the cove where they had dressed. Gil sank into the darkness behind the fire lay.

Tasha felt her way in the darkness, holding tight to Raina's hand. There was a jumble of rocks at the rear of the little cove. She crouched behind them, shielding Raina with her body.

She didn't have to tell the little girl to be quiet. Her small body was trembling with fear. Silently Tasha stroked Raina's hair, willing herself to be calm and stay hidden while every nerve screamed that she should run, fight, do anything but remain still in the darkness. There was another echo of a falling rock. Whoever had entered the cave did not know the way. Ari would have moved silently. Tasha felt her arms tighten around the child and she forced herself to relax.

Slowly the minutes ticked by. Tasha shifted her weight, resting her back against a large boulder, cradling Raina in her arms. As she strained to listen, Tasha gradually became aware of the murmur of voices, audible over the quiet gurgle of the underground stream. Instinctively she put her hand over Raina's mouth and felt the little head nod in understanding.

She thought of the rock where she had cut out Gil's clothes. Had she removed all of the cloth? Had she carelessly dropped a piece and then not noticed it in the darkness? She had put away the needle and thread. The knife she still carried, slipped into the waistband of the borrowed trousers. The pack had been tossed to the back of the cove, jumbled in with the furs, blankets, and extra clothing. Where was Gil? Had he managed to hide?

The light of a torch reflected off the walls and ceiling of the cavern. She could understand some of the words now: "wild-goose chase," "never find their way in here," "have to search," "kitchen boy"...

She could recognize some of the voices, too. They were the guards from the compound. Olaf was one of them. He was doing most of the talking and seemed to be in charge.

Even with her eyes closed, Tasha could sense the light from the torches as absolute blackness gave way before them. As the intruders entered the cavern, she no longer had to strain to understand what they were saying.

"I tell you they never could have gotten in here." It was the cook speaking. "You would have to be born around here to even know these caves exist."

There was a pause, then a shuffle, as someone rubbed his foot in the sand near the water. Olaf's voice echoed through the cavern. "Oh, no? Look at this. Footprints. And this. Someone has put out a torch here by rubbing it in the sand."

"Watch out." It was the cook speaking again. "There's quicksand and dropoffs in this room. You wait here and let me take a look around. I've been in and out of this cave since I was a kid. If you had let me lead coming in you wouldn't have gone stumbling all over those rocks and let everyone and his friend know we were coming."

Tasha could see the reflection of a light advancing to the cove where Gil was hiding. There was some shuffling, a grunt, and the light receded.

"They've been here, all right," the cook said again, "at least the kitchen boy has. Here's part of his old shirt. It's been ripped apart. No one around now, though. Probably took off early this morning. See this stick? Part of a fire lay, but it's cold as ice."

"How do we know they ain't hidin' somewhere in some other tunnel?" Olaf asked.

"Them tunnels on the other side lead back around into dead ends. You can hear where the water goes down a waterfall and back underground." The flickering reflections began to dim, and the cook started back down the tunnel, still talking, leading the others after him. "Can't swim across that river to the other side. It's too deep and the water's so cold your muscles cramp up right away. Me and my friend crossed it, though. Drug some logs down here and made ourselves a raft..."

Tasha sat for a long time after the voices had dimmed

and gone. As she gradually relaxed, she felt Raina do the same, until the child's quiet breathing told her that she was asleep. Then she heard a quiet rustle.

"Tasha, Raina!" Gil whispered, his voice coming in their direction.

"Here," Tasha answered. "We're back here."

Tasha reached out into the blackness and found Gil's hand, feeling after the sound of her voice. She guided him around the boulder and pulled him down beside her.

"Do you think they're gone?" he asked.

"I think so, but we'd better stay hidden just the same."

She shifted her weight and laid Raina on the sand, resting her head in her lap. "The cook found your shirt. I shouldn't have been so careless. But it seemed almost as if he were leading the others away from us."

"He was." Gil's voice trembled and Tasha felt him shudder. "He saw me."

VIII

"He *saw* you?" Tasha nearly forgot to whisper.

"Yes. I was hiding in the furs and blankets. My head wasn't all the way covered and I didn't dare move. I opened my eyes and he was looking at me. He picked up a blanket and tossed it over my head. Then he must have picked up one of the sticks from last night's fire before he went back to the others."

"Is he one of Marko's followers? What do you know about him? Do you think Ari trusts him?"

"He never said much to me. I never saw him much when we lived in the inn, before the king had us sent to the compound. Then we both had to work in the kitchen, and he would yell at me when one of the guards was around. Sometimes he would pretend to beat me, but it never hurt much. He's big. I was always surprised that his beatings didn't hurt. Then, after Ari came he let me go hunting with him."

"Here, Gil," Tasha passed the sleeping Raina to him; then, feeling her way in the inky blackness, she made her way around the rocks and into the next cove. As she was gathering up some blankets and furs, her hand touched one of the packs that Ari had stored along the wall. Reaching her hand down inside she found something that felt like dried meat. She slipped the straps over her shoulder, picked up the blankets again, and felt her way back to Gil and Raina.

Clearing away the stones as best she could, she made a bed for Raina, then covered herself with one of the blankets, handed another to Gil and started to explore the pack. There were small packets of dried meat inside. She gave one to Gil, who attacked it hungrily.

The meat was well dried and hard to chew. Ari had used hickory wood to smoke it and had seasoned it with salt. There was even a taste of black pepper. Though a steady diet of it would soon become monotonous, Tasha found that she liked the flavor. Tucked into the corner of the pack was a small container of water. As she satisfied her hunger and thirst, she felt herself relaxing under the warmth of the blanket. It was easier to close her eyes than to strain to see in the absolute blackness and soon she joined Raina and the now-sleeping Gil, dozing off into a world of strange dreams of storms and figures striding out of the blackness, silhouetted in dancing torchlight.

It was the light from Ari's torch that awakened her. He listened soberly as she and Gil related their experience with the searchers. There was an understanding nod when Gil told him about the cook and how he had led the searchers back to the mouth of the cave.

"What do you think?" Tasha asked, adding another stick to the small fire Ari had kindled in their old spot. "Will they be back? Did the cook lead them away to help us or is he just waiting to turn us in himself? There's probably some kind of reward being offered."

Ari was silent a long time, adding carrots and potatoes to the stew now boiling on the coals. Tasha was finding it hard to conceal her impatience when he finally answered.

"The cook was the one who told me about this cave. I should have known he would lead the others in a search here. But I don't think he will betray us. He has too much at stake."

He looked at Gil as he spoke and Tasha sensed that there was something more behind his words than he had voiced. There was a reason why the cook had not betrayed Gil. Even more than that, there was something between Ari and the cook. Something old and deep that reached back into the past. She could see it in Ari's expression as he looked at the boy. Somehow the incident in the cave had ripped open an old wound.

"Still," Ari said, closing his eyes briefly as if to close the door on the old memories, "we need to be watchful. I had hoped to use the cave until the search had extended away from here." He looked briefly at Raina. "It will be hard on the child to travel as fast as we need to in such cold and dampness. But perhaps the cook has done his work well enough. If they have searched here and not found us, then there is no reason to return and search again. Come, let us eat."

In spite of their earlier snack, Tasha found that she was ravenous. Gil, too, made short work of the heaping bowl of food Ari gave him. Little Raina, who had slept through their meal of jerky was especially hungry. But she stopped and handed back her bowl before it was empty.

Tasha opened her mouth to urge her to eat more. The child was too thin and the months of work among the lint and dust in the weaving rooms had given her a cough that would never quite go away. Ari saw what Tasha was about to do and raised his finger to silence her.

"See what I was able to find for my special friend," he said to Raina.

He pulled a paper from his pocket and carefully unwrapped it.

Tasha gasped, "A chocolate bar! Where on earth did you ever find such a thing? I haven't seen one of those since Com gained power." She looked at Raina and then back at Ari. "I doubt Raina even remembers what it is. We limited her sweets at the palace, and there have been none at all at the compound."

"Oh, there are such things at the compound, if you know where to look or whom to talk to," Ari replied.

"I remember chocolate," Gil said, eyeing the small slab. "Before I was taken to the compound, a daughter of one of the royalists who lived in the house where I worked slipped me a piece. It was delicious. She made me wash my face as soon as I ate it so that no one would suspect she had given it to me. I think her father might have beaten her if he had known."

Ari listened with a sad smile, then carefully broke off a small square and handed it to Gil, who wolfed it down with a smile.

Raina watched Gil's satisfied expression, then asked, "May I have some, too?"

Ari broke off another piece. "Of course little one. I will set it here on this clean stone and as soon as you are finished eating, the piece is yours."

"But I am finished," she protested.

Ari looked at her bowl, then picked it up and handed it back. "Food is very hard to get, and very important if we are to have the strength to go to your brother. Eat what is in the bowl and then you may have the chocolate."

Raina looked at him a long while, her eyes large in her thin face. Then, without another word, she picked up her spoon and finished the rest of the stew.

"Now?" she said reaching for the chocolate.

"Now," Ari answered with a smile. "Enjoy it."

It was impossible to tell day from night in the blackness of the cave. Ari came and went, always fixing large pots of stew for them to warm and eat in his absence. The chamber was large. The stream was fed by a clear spring on the left of the entrance tunnel. Ari gave careful instructions that drinking jugs were to be filled directly from the spring, not further down the stream. Though there didn't seem to be any bats in this part of the cave, they were in other parts, and he did not want to risk any sickness that might be carried in their droppings.

Though most of the cave floor was limestone, some parts, like their little coves, were covered with sand. Past the coves, a short way into another tunnel, the floor was mud. Here Ari, or someone, perhaps the cook and his friend, had dug out a latrine.

When Ari would leave, Tasha would extinguish the torch he always left burning, and would allow only a small fire to be lit in the cove. Always, she would talk barely above a whisper, and Gil and Raina, though they talked and giggled and made up stories, spoke quietly. Each day as the hours passed following Ari's departure, Tasha felt the tension grow inside her, winding ever tighter, like the spring in a clock. Only when he would return, build up the fire, light the torches again, and start to cook would she allow herself to relax.

"Why is the room always in darkness when I return?" Ari asked one evening as he methodically sliced a turnip into the pot.

"We always keep it dark so the bad men won't find us," Raina answered before Tasha could speak.

He looked at Tasha sharply. "It isn't good for the children to always be in darkness."

"Well, what are we supposed to do?" Tasha couldn't hold back the flow of words. "You leave, never telling us where you are going or when you will be back. You have never told us what to expect, what is happening out there. I don't even know where we are. What if someday they catch you and you don't come back? Which way do we go? We can't even tell if it's night or day. We are as much your prisoners in this cave as we ever were in the compound."

At this last statement she saw hurt and then anger pass through Ari's eyes. His jaw clenched and the knuckles holding the knife went white. She braced herself for a sharp retort, but then she saw the jaw relax and he resumed slicing the turnip into the pot.

Gil and Raina had inched backward under her onslaught and sat now with their backs against the packs, their arms around each other.

Suddenly she felt drained. She blinked to hold back the tears. "I'm sorry. I shouldn't have said that. But it's so hard, sitting in the darkness, never knowing . . ."

"You're right," Ari said at last. "I haven't been fair to you. Marko sent me on this mission to take you out of the country, not only because he wants you both out of danger, but also as a sign."

"A sign?"

"Yes, the people know you. They loved your father and now that he is gone, they have transferred that love to you. There aren't many who knew you were in the compound, not of the common people. The royalists have started rumors. Some that you were killed, others that you secretly plotted against Marko and are siding with the royalists." He paused, then added, "Some even that you are now the hidden mistress of the king himself."

Tasha gasped and felt the blood drain from her face.

"Everyone knows that something has recently happened," Ari continued. "Suddenly there are soldiers everywhere, searching barns, woods, abandoned houses, and even haystacks. The people, of course, have been told nothing, but they are beginning to learn what has happened."

"You mean, they are finding out about our escape?"

"Yes." Ari picked up a wooden spoon and started to stir the thick stew. "There are many who are members of the underground, but each one knows only one or two others. I have been contacting the ones I know and have started to spread the word that you have escaped."

"But what good will that do?"

"It will alert some who will be ready to help us, but that is not the main reason they must know. The people know that when the White Dove has flown safely away, then it will not be long until Marko returns with his army. As I said, it is a sign."

Gil spoke from the shadows, "So what are we to do?"

Ari started ladling the stew into their bowls. "I'm sorry, but for a time you must remain hidden. There are certain papers stored in the home the king has recently taken for his own. I think it will be invaluable if we take them with us when we leave. I have gathered enough supplies to keep you for a while. I will arrange it so that if something happens to me, the cook will find a way to return and let you know to go on alone."

Tasha felt as if a great weight had descended upon her shoulders. She could see the same thing reflected in the faces of Raina and Gil. More time in the cave. More days in the darkness. And now they wouldn't even have the relief of Ari's comings and goings.

"I don't think we can do it, Ari." Tasha tried to speak around the lump in her throat. "More days in the darkness..."

"You will *have* to do it." Ari's voice was strange and harsh. "Where is the fine strong girl Marko told me about? The one who would never falter?"

Tasha ate in silence for a few minutes, her mind racing with thoughts. Finishing the stew, she held out her bowl for another helping. "Ari," she began, hoping her voice did not betray her. "You forget, Com has been in contact with me. Don't try to shield me from what I already know. He is living in my old home."

Ari paused, the brimming ladle only halfway to the bowl. Finally he filled the bowl and handed it back to her. "Yes, Com is living in your father's house. I should have realized that you would know."

Tasha spooned the stew into her mouth quickly and set down the bowl with a determined *thump*. "Then it is settled. We will go with you to find the papers."

IX

ARI LOOKED AT HER NARROWLY. "THAT IS OUT OF THE QUESTION. You must wait here until I return."

"Ari." Tasha tried to keep her voice from pleading. "Ari, how many times have you been in that house?"

He shrugged. "I know the house well enough. I was there to talk to Marko, before the revolution."

"Then he met you in his office or in the salon. Am I right?"

Ari nodded. "I met him in the office."

"A meeting in the office tells you nothing about that house. You have no idea where something might be hidden."

"I know that house better than you might suppose. I will find what I am looking for."

"You will look in the lockbox in the office and find nothing. Then what will you do?"

"I doubt the papers I am searching for will be in the office. There may be important ones there, but the ones I really want are hidden in the secret compartment that is behind the panel in the bedroom suite of the west wing."

Tasha opened her eyes wide. "How did you know of that?" Anxious to tell her father something, Tasha had rushed in on him one day to find him carefully placing a small packet in the open compartment. She knew from his expression she must not mention it to anyone. Not until shortly before his death did he teach her how it was opened.

"How I know is not important. What is important is, does Com know of it?"

"You forget. Com was one of the young men my father sponsored at the academy. He spent many hours in the house. Father trusted him and refused to think that any of his scholars, especially Com, would turn against him. He made him privy to many things; it is very possible that he also told him of the secret compartment, but I don't know for sure."

"Still, that is where the papers we want are hidden, unless Com has found and destroyed them." Ari paused and looked at Tasha closely. "This Com, how well do you really know him?"

She twined her fingers together in her lap. "He's always wanted to marry me. You've seen how he still comes to ask. He thought he would, in the end, in spite of my feelings. When Marko came he was very bitter."

"So, if you do come with me, what do we do with the children?"

"They must not stay here alone. I know where we can

leave them. Like the cook, I too know many hiding places. We will go mad, hiding always in the dark."

Ari thought for a long time, then shook his head. "It is too dangerous. If you cannot stand the darkness, I will take you to another spot I have prepared. But you cannot come into the very heart of the Capital."

"But I must go with you." Tasha's voice was insistent. "What would take you hours to find, I can do in minutes."

She smiled and looked directly into his eyes. "You are silent and leave no tracks in the wilderness. I doubt you will do as well in my father's house. You must at least consider it."

"Do not be so sure. As I said, I know that house well enough. Still, I will consider it, but I will not promise more."

Ari was gone when Tasha awoke. Gone too were several of the blankets and one of the smaller packs. Strangely, she felt no anger.

Somehow she was sure that this disappearance was just part of the preparations for their journey. He would return before going to the Capital.

Tasha draped a blanket over some rocks to shield the sleeping children from the light, and built up the fire. She pulled out some coals and set the leftover stew on to warm. Then, deciding she could at least have a look around, she took one of the torches from the pile Ari had made and lit it. The stream was narrow right below the spring. Tasha propped up the torch in a crack between some rocks, found a flat stone, and heaved it into the middle of the stream. Now she could easily cross to the other side.

Not far from the stream, she found a hollowed-out basin as large as the tub in her old home. With a cry of delight she touched her hair, suddenly feeling very dirty. She re-crossed the stream and hurried to the fire. The children were awake and watching her. She noticed that Gil had already dished out bowls of stew for himself and Raina. Hurriedly, she scraped the remainder of stew from the pot and set it aside.

"Aren't you going to eat?" Raina asked.

"Better than that. Today we're all going to have a bath!"

It would be easiest to heat the water near the natural basin. While she carried the torch and lugged the heavy pot, the children followed, arms full of firewood. She heated a little water and then, using some sand and a piece of Gil's old shirt, scoured out the cooking pot, then filled it with water and set it to heat.

It would take forever to heat enough for them to have a real bath, but they could fill the basin enough so they could wash their hair and scrub all over.

She went back to the campsite. She and Raina were still wearing the trousers and shirts Ari had given them the first night. Now she pulled out a dress for Raina and an extra skirt and blouse that she had brought in her bundle. There was a large bar of lye soap that they had used to wash their hands and faces. It wasn't like the sweet smelling soap she had had growing up, but it would clean.

"Gil." Her voice was filled with the energy that comes from finally doing something constructive. "While Raina and I bathe, shake out the blankets and furs and roll them up. Use those rawhide strips to tie them. We must be ready to go when Ari comes."

She found a coarse towel and a rag to use for a washcloth and returned to the other fire where Raina was waiting. Twice she filled the drinking jug from the stream and emptied it into the basin, then she added enough of the hot water to warm the rest. The darkness itself gave them the privacy they needed. Raina shivered as Tasha scrubbed her, finishing with a rinse of warm water from the jug.

"Now," Tasha said as she finished dressing Raina in her clean clothes, "take the torch and go join Gil by the fire."

She added some more water from the stream and then recklessly added the rest of the pot of hot water. Filling the cooking pot once more from the stream, she set it on the fire to warm for Gil.

How delicious to wash away the grime and smoke! Even with the warm water, her teeth were chattering in the cold of the cave before she finished, but Tasha didn't care. Repeatedly she scrubbed her cropped hair, rinsing it over and over. Finally she grabbed the towel and rubbed herself dry. How wonderful to dress in clean clothes!

She knelt by the basin and washed her clothes and Raina's, rinsing them in the cold water of the stream.

"Here, Gil." Tasha handed him one of their eating

bowls. "Use this to dip out the dirty water. We should wash those clothes."

Gil held out a small bundle. "I found some clothes of Ari's. I can wear them until mine are dry." He grinned. "Don't worry. I have washed my own clothes for a long time."

Tasha hung the damp clothes on the rocks near the fire. By the time Ari returned, they were nearly dry, the cooking pot was back and filled with food, and corn cakes were baking on a flat stone.

"What? You are not huddled together in the darkness. I have been replaced as cook and much of my soap, I suspect, is gone."

"Tasha found a tub, and we all had a bath. Even Gil."

"I hope you don't mind," Gil said. "I borrowed some of your clothes. Just until mine are dry."

"What's this?" Ari asked. "Sleeping blankets and robes rolled and tied. Is someone planning on leaving?"

"We all are," Tasha said, more forcefully than she expected. "We need to stay together. We won't slow you down and we *can* help."

Ari held up his hand. "Yes, I've considered it carefully. We will go together, but not tonight. There are still contacts that have to be made, still some preparations we have to complete. That, I must do alone."

"But how long...?"

"There is not much left to do. Possibly two or three days. You still must trust me. Agreed?"

"Agreed. Tell us when we are going and we will be ready. In the meantime"—Tasha paused and smiled—"there is a nice basin on the other side of the stream. After supper we will be happy to heat some more water."

Ari met her smile with one of his own. "Yes—*after* supper."

X

TASHA HAD FINISHED COVERING THE SLEEPING Raina when Ari motioned her over to the fire. He glanced at Gil, who was also breathing heavily, then withdrew a paper from a pocket inside his vest.

"You were right. You need to know where we are and where we are going. I secured this map. It is an old one, of the old republic, the names have been changed, but even the mighty royalists have not been able to relocate the cities and towns."

"Here"—Ari pointed—"in the middle of what is now the 'Royal Game Preserve,' is the location of the compound. We crossed the river here, just downstream from where it makes this bend. The cave is in the hills here, west of the Reed River."

"Good. I'd hoped that's where we were."

"Why? We're nearly fifty miles from the Capital, we have

to backtrack all of that way and then go nearly another two hundred miles north to the Great North River."

"It's because of Raina. In spite of the better diet, she still is not strong. And it hasn't helped that we have stayed here so long without exercise. Tell me, does this cave have some sort of opening onto the other side of this range of hills? We entered the cave on the west slope, yet you always go and come from the other side of the cavern. Are you using another entrance on the east side?"

"Yes, the other entrance comes out about here."

"Wonderful!" Tasha was smiling now.

"The terrain here is very rocky, with thick underbrush. It will not be easier on the child."

"Ari, have they stopped searching for us?"

"They are still looking but things are beginning to calm down. I think they believe we left on the raft."

"Then perhaps it will work." Tasha paused, studying the map.

"What are you looking for?"

"It's here," she said pointing to the map, "outside of El-more, or whatever it is called now. There is a large farm owned by Amoz."

"I know the place."

"Amoz is married to my mother's sister Marta. Their oldest daughter, Lora, and I were like sisters growing up. Amoz is silly and pompous and I hear he has sided with the royalists to save his property, but he would never betray us. They have many children, one near the age of Raina.

She could stay with them and I think she would not be discovered."

"You're right. With all of those children, Raina would fit right in. She even looks like their younger daughters. The journey would not be far, it would take only a little more than a day."

"You know Amoz and Marta?"

"Amoz and his family have been my friends for many years. Openly he has sided with the king, but he is one of our most reliable and important contacts. Even the children can be counted on to pass along information accurately and discretely. Shortly after you were taken to the compound, Lora crossed the river and joined our forces there. Amoz insisted she leave for her own safety."

Tasha rocked back on her heels. "But I never heard them mention the name of Ari."

"I have known Amoz for many years, but I only lived in this area a short while just prior to my marriage. I have come to know Marta as well, though we have rarely spoken face to face. Since our escape, I have been in contact with Ben, the oldest boy at home. The others I have seen from a distance. Ben knows of the plan to steal the papers. He does not know you are with me, but I think he suspects the truth. Once he asked about you. I just said to pass on the word that the White Dove had flown."

Raina stirred in her sleep and Tasha pulled the blanket back up over her shoulders. "What about Gil?" she asked.

"There is a lot of work on a farm during spring planting.

I do not think an extra boy would be noticed," Ari said and nodded. "You have a good plan. The children will be safe there, and they will be taken care of if something happens to us."

Ari folded up the map. "It is late." He paused and the corners of his eyes crinkled in a smile, "and someone has ordered me to have a bath before I can rest."

Tasha laughed softly and handed him the bar of soap. "Sleep well."

Ari was gone again the next morning when Tasha awoke. There was a pot of stew simmering over some coals and corn cakes ready to be baked. He had left the map, so after breakfast she sat down with Gil and Raina and they studied it together. She showed them where the cave was, pointed out the direction they would leave, and talked to them of major towns and landmarks. Without saying so directly, she made sure they knew the way to the Great North River crossing, where Marko and others loyal to the republic were waiting for them.

When Ari returned he brought good news. The weather was mild, the ground was firm, and they would be able to leave. They set to work at once, packing, sorting, and dividing their supplies. Some, including potatoes, carrots, and turnips and a supply of jerky, would be left in the cave as an emergency storage in case they had to return and hide. The best fur pelts would be given to Amoz and Marta to sell or trade for supplies. The worst of their clothing they burned. The rest they divided into packs, each containing a change of clothes and a supply of dried meat. Carefully Tasha transferred the precious bone hairpins to her personal pack. Some of the packs would be hidden in a cache not far from the Amoz farm. The others they would take with them.

It was late when they finished, but before going to bed, Tasha took Raina on her lap, Ari sat with his hand on Gil's shoulder, and they asked God to bless them in their journey. Then they slept. When they awoke they would leave.

XI

ASHA WAS SURPRISED WHEN THEY LEFT THE HIDDEN entrance on the other side of the cave to find, not the bright sunlight she expected, but the darkness of night, the pale glow of a sliver of moon, and a heaven full of stars. In the cave she had assumed that Ari was leaving at dawn and returning in the evening, but it was only logical that he would do his scouting, hunting, and making contacts during the night, under cover of darkness.

They made slow progress down the hillside. In all his comings and goings, Ari told her, he had tried never to use the same way twice so as to lessen the chance that someone might follow him to the hidden entrance. The lack of a trail and the heavy packs held them back, and Tasha could not help pausing to look up at the stars massed in the sky.

It was near dawn when Ari led them into a clearing in the midst of a dense thicket of evergreens, where they shed the heavy packs, ate a little dried meat, and soon fell asleep.

Tasha could tell by the position of the sun that it was late afternoon when she awoke. The spring sun filtered through the trees. She found a bright spot and let its rays bathe her face with warmth and light. How good it felt after the long days of hiding in the dark of the cave. A breeze ruffled the leaves on the trees, bringing with it the scent of wild plumb blossoms. Overhead a robin sang, and from a nearby thicket she could hear the coo of a dove.

It was on a day like this that she had found the little white dove with its injured wing. She must have been only about as old as Raina. Her father's big dogs terrified her and the barn cats were too wild to tame. The bird became her pet, and she took it with her everywhere, even when she would accompany her father on his many tours throughout the kingdom. Old Samuel fixed a nest box for it among the pigeon-post birds, but she preferred to carry it about with her in a basket, lined with scraps of silk and wool. In time, it would even ride about on her shoulder.

"But you, my Tasha," her father would say, gathering her up in his arms, "you are *my* little dove." The name stuck. Though only her father ever called her that to her face, when Ari spread the word that the White Dove had flown, the people knew of whom he spoke.

A rabbit hopped across the clearing and paused to nibble on a patch of spring grass. Tasha watched it until Gil stirred, frightening it away. She took the map out of her pocket and studied it, trying to pinpoint their location. It was no good. The map was not detailed enough to be of much help. The hill they were on sloped to the east and south. How far they had come, or how much farther it was to the Amoz farm, she could not tell.

The red glow of sunset was lighting the sky when the children finally awoke. Ari had awakened soon after Tasha and had gone, returning with fresh water and a bowl of tender greens, a welcome addition to their diet of dried meat.

As soon as they had finished eating they shouldered their packs and followed Ari into the darkness of the wooded hills. After the pitch black of the cave, Tasha found this darkness at once friendlier and more disconcerting. Now there were shapes and shadows everywhere. At times Ari would pause, listen carefully, and sometimes change direction. Once he quickly guided them into a deep ravine while something above crashed past in the undergrowth. Whether it was someone on patrol or an animal hunting for food or fleeing the hunter Tasha did not know. No one spoke. They didn't have enough energy for that. When the noise had died away and Ari was satisfied that it was safe to go on, he helped them up and out, and they resumed their march.

As the stars began to fade, Ari led them to a hunting lodge, nestled on the edge of a small clearing. They waited in the fringe of trees while he checked it out, then entered. There was a fireplace, laid with wood and ready for a fire, but they dared not set it alight. Instead, they breakfasted again on jerky and cold water.

Here, someone would have to keep watch. Tasha asked for the first watch. Even as tired as she was, she could not wait to see the sunrise and experience the freshness of the early morning. It was midmorning when Ari emerged from the doorway and came to relieve her. She knew he had not rested enough, but she was too tired to argue, and went inside and fell asleep on the hard bunk at once.

It was nearly evening when she awoke. Ari was again asleep on the bunk on the other side of the cabin. From a crack in a shutter she made out the form of Gil, watching and listening, and rubbing his eyes to stave off sleep.

Before she could go out and send the boy back inside, Ari awoke, and once more they had to shoulder the heavy packs. This time, night had only begun when Ari called a halt. Leaving them hidden in another thicket of evergreens, he stepped out alone into the woods and was soon swallowed from view.

When he returned, Ben was with him and guided them down the last slope of the hill, across a hay field, and into the cellar door of the farmhouse.

Ben slid aside a shelf, filled with boxes and bales of supplies, and led them into a hidden room. There were bunks against a wall, a table and chairs in the middle of the room, and an oil lamp hanging from the ceiling for light. The walls were covered with colorful fabric and a woven rug nearly covered the floor. A small stove stood in the corner, its chimney connected to the chimney of the main house so the smoke would not be noticeable. Ben opened the cupboards and showed them extra blankets as well as a large supply of food: dried fruits, vegetables, and a large store of nuts, already shelled. In a separate bathroom, water ran in through a pipe, filled a basin, and ran out through a covered ditch into a drain field.

Ben disappeared for a few minutes and returned with a tray holding a large pitcher of milk, fresh bread, newly churned butter, a salad of tender leaf lettuce and small radishes, and a large dish of meat and vegetable pie. There was even a small pot of honey for the bread, which was still warm from the oven.

Tasha opened her mouth to speak, but Ari held up his hand and his eyes warned her to silence. They washed quickly and before Ben had finished transferring all of the dishes to the table, they were ready to eat. Without anyone's saying a word, Ben lit the lamp, then left, securing the secret door behind him.

"Why didn't you let me talk to him?" Tasha asked. "Does Marta know we are here? Have you talked to them about our plans?"

Maddeningly slow as always, Ari carefully finished buttering a piece of bread before he answered. "All Marta and Amoz know is that four strangers, fleeing the royalists, need a place to stop for a few days. When things are settled for the night, I will slip outside with Ben and present our plan to Amoz, at least part of it. He will not know who you are, or where we are going. Of course, he will recognize Raina so he will doubtless figure out that you were here. Marta will be told only about Raina and Gil. And of the children, only Ben will know the rest. That way, when they are questioned, it will be easier for them. If troops come to scour the farm and question people, Ben will disappear with Gil. Raina, of course, will just pass as one of their own children."

Gil stopped eating and looked hard at Ari. "You mean I am not going with you?"

Ari looked at Tasha in surprise. "Don't the children know what is going on?"

She shook her head. "No, I didn't know how much to tell them. We only discussed the map and the way to the Great North River. I didn't say anything to them of the rest."

Ari turned to Raina. "Listen carefully, and never tell *anyone* what I am about to tell you, or we may never be together again. Tasha and I are going to be gone for a few days to pick up some important things that Marko needs very much. We will have to go fast, and it would be hard to keep up. For that reason we are leaving you here to wait for us."

Raina looked around at the tiny room and her lip began to tremble.

Tasha put her arm around the little girl and smiled.

"Not here in this room, Raina. Here on this farm. Do you remember, before the war, when we went to see Marta and Lora and Jewel and Beka?"

Raina smiled and nodded. She had only been four years old at the time, but the trip and the days of fun playing with Marta's girls on the farm had made a great impression on her and she still remembered.

"Well," Tasha continued, "Lora is grown up and moved away, but Jewel and Beka still live here with Aunt Marta and Uncle Amoz. For the next while, until I come back, you are going to live here too and pretend that Jewel and Beka and Ben and all the others are your brothers and sisters."

"But where will you be?"

"I am going with Ari. Marko needs some things that we can get for him. It is a special present that will make him very happy. Will you stay here so that Ari and I can get that present for Marko?"

Raina nodded. Though her face was drawn and her eyes wide and filling with tears, she blinked them back and nodded again. "All right," she whispered.

"Remember, it is very important that you tell anyone who asks you that Jewel and Beka are your sisters and that Marta and Amoz are your mama and papa."

"What about me?" Gil asked, his attention temporarily diverted from the food piled on his plate.

Ari's big hand came to rest on Gil's shoulder. "You have a very important part in this mission. It is to stay here and look after Raina."

He gave Tasha a meaningful glance and she rose from the table, taking Raina by the hand.

"Look, Raina, you have a spot of gravy on your dress. Let's hurry in and wash it out before it makes a stain."

In the bathroom, Raina started to play in the water. Tasha, standing by the door, heard Ari continue. "There is a very real chance that Tasha and I will not return from this mission. As Marko's sister, Raina would be a most important hostage to the royalists. Though I know Marta and Amoz will not refuse to care for her when they know she is here, just having her here puts them and their family in great danger."

He broke off another piece of bread and started to butter it carefully. "If we do not return, stay here as long as you can. If Raina's presence becomes a danger to the family, it will be up to you to get her through the country and across the Great North River to her brother. It may not seem like a very important assignment, baby-sitting a little girl, but it is a very valuable service indeed and means a lot to the movement of the democratic republic. There are those who will help you. Amoz is one. The cook in the compound is another who will do all he can for you."

Gil started to speak, but Ari held up his hand. "While there is a very real chance we will not return, there are also many things that say we will. There will be plenty of time, after we have crossed the river to safety, for you to serve your republic in more exciting ways. We need your help, Gil. Will you do it?"

Gil looked up. He glanced over his shoulder and saw Tasha watching him. Behind her, Raina played happily in the water. He squared his shoulders. "I'll do it, Ari. You don't have to worry."

Tasha smiled and turned back to the little girl, but not before she noticed a strange expression pass over Ari's face and his hand tighten on Gil's shoulder.

They stayed in the underground room all the rest of that night and the next day. Ari left for a short while, and when he returned, Tasha knew that the arrangements had been finalized for Raina and Gil.

During the afternoon, Tasha rested as much as she could. They would travel as they had been doing, walking at night and resting during the day. They would stay as much as possible to the wilderness areas and avoid roads and houses. It would not be an easy journey.

Finally they heard the house settle down for the night and Ben came to lead them out of their hiding place. Gil would sleep with the farmworkers in a bunkhouse near the barn. Raina would share a bed with her new "sisters."

Tasha hugged the child close, fighting back the tears that stung her eyes, trying to smile and pretend that this was just part of a great adventure. Since that first day when Marko had appeared, lugging his baby sister, she had loved and cared for the orphan girl. Even in the good times they had hardly been apart. She could feel the slight frame tremble in her embrace.

"Hurry back, Tasha." The voice was barely above a

whisper. "I can't wait to go so we can give your surprise to Marko." She attempted a crooked smile.

"We will," Tasha managed to whisper. "Now remember, until Ari and I return, Marta is your mama, Amoz is your papa, and Gil will be here to watch out for you." She gave the child another squeeze. "Give me another kiss and go with Ben, your new big brother."

Tasha hugged her once more, fiercely. Then she kissed her, put her small hand into Ben's large one, and gave her a little push. "Remember always," she managed to whisper, "I love you very much."

Raina turned quickly to give Tasha another hug and kiss on the cheek. "I love you, too." Then she walked out the door with Ben, repeating, "Marta is my mama, and Amoz is my papa."

For a long time Tasha knelt there on the floor, letting her tears flow freely. Ari and Gil sat together on one of the bunks. She was vaguely aware of Ari's voice, full of emotion, talking quietly to Gil, but she was so overcome with her own feelings that she did not pay any attention to what he was saying. Finally, she rose and went in to wash the tears from her face. When she returned to the main room, Ben was back. He had deposited Raina with her new sisters, he said, and left her snuggled up in bed with Jewel, a new doll clutched in her arms.

For the first time, Tasha noticed that Gil was crying and Ari's eyes were also full of tears. Man and boy embraced each other and then Gil left with Ben for his new quarters.

Tasha wondered what had passed between the two of them, but one look at Ari's face and she knew it was something too personal, that she should not pry. Instead she turned and shouldered her pack. Ari did the same, and when Ben returned again, they were ready to follow him out of the shelter of the house, into the darkness of the woods beyond.

XII

THEY MADE GOOD TIME. THEIR HEAVY PACKS HAD been replaced with small light ones carrying only a change of clothes, a blanket, and a day's supply of food for each of them. It would be replenished from hidden caches along the way. Tasha wore a man's hat and the trousers and shirt she had used in the cave. In her pack she carried the bone hairpins and a dress Ben had given her. It would be more suitable for walking around in the capital city.

Word had been sent through the underground that two travelers would be needing food along the way, and arrangements were made for someone to meet them at each cache and direct them to the next stop. Each time, it was Ari who met the contact. Tasha stayed well back in the shadows, never speaking, trying to appear as much as possible like a male companion. Soldiers were still looking for a man and a girl together, accompanied by two children, a boy of about twelve and a girl between six and eight years old. Stymied in their efforts to quickly and quietly recapture Tasha and the others, the royalists had finally resorted to the offer of a reward to influence someone to turn them in. Fliers asking for their return were posted in most public places. Anything they could do to distance themselves from this description, the more likely their chance of success.

It took them four nights of travel to reach the Capital. Though they were able to travel at a steady pace, their roundabout route through woods, always skirting towns and villages, added miles and made their trip more difficult. It had been only two years since Com had taken over, but mismanagement and war had taken their toll on the countryside. The neat forest paths and well-groomed fields Tasha remembered from her childhood were now choked with weeds and undergrowth.

It was a few hours before dawn when they came in sight of the city. Street lamps along the main thoroughfare made pinpricks of light against the dark. Shadows of the government buildings could be seen against the skyline.

They stopped to rest in a dense grove of trees in one of the many hunting preserves that the royalists had created for the enjoyment of the governing elite. If they were caught there, they would be arrested for trespassing, but travel too near the city in the hours before dawn carried an even greater penalty.

An early morning fog lay dense along the Paulos River,

which meandered through the fields on the edge of the city. When the darkness began to fade before the first rays of sunrise, Ari and Tasha left the shelter of the grove and traveled quickly down the hill and into the protecting cover of mist.

Now it was time for Tasha to take the lead. They walked east along the bank of the Paulos River until it curved to the south around the city. The banks here were steeper and closer together, and sometime in the distant past someone had built a picturesque footbridge. Now rarely used and nearly hidden by a tangle of vines and blackberry brambles, its cedar posts were nonetheless still sound. On the other side, a small path led back toward the west. It was this path that Tasha followed, her feelings alternating between excitement and apprehension.

They stopped under a large oak tree. A path led toward a bungalow nestled in a small grove of trees just outside the city proper. Tasha pointed to the house, saying, "There, that is the home of my old governess. If she still lives, she will help us."

The mist was starting to burn off, and, as they approached the house, they could see neat rows of newly planted flowers on each side of a gravel path. The gravel had been recently raked. On the south side of the house a garden spot was in the process of being readied for spring planting.

Tasha smiled. "Ana is alive. Only she could make a yard look like that." She walked boldly up the path, listened for a minute at the front door, then skirted around the house to the back.

Before she could knock, Ari stepped forward. "Let me talk to her first. Someone may suspect that you would come here. She may have visitors."

Ari's knock was answered almost immediately. "Yes? May I help you?"

"We are two travelers who seek only a meal and a place to rest for a few hours. May we come in?"

Before she could answer, Tasha stepped forward and pulled off the hat covering her head, revealing her face.

Ana's surprise was complete. Quickly she glanced around toward the rows of raspberries and lilac bushes that bordered her property in the back and separated it from the city wall. Then she opened the door wider, stepped aside, and pulled them both into the house.

After bolting the door she turned and with a cry flung her arms around Tasha. "Tasha, my Tasha, you are still alive! When I heard they were looking for a woman I wondered. But why are you here? And what about Raina? Is she all right? You cannot stay in the city. They are searching everywhere for you. Already they have searched my house many times. They suspect you may come here."

She gave Tasha another hug. "Oh, Tasha, I am so glad that you are alive. Here, let me give you something to eat. Sit. The water is already hot, I'll just add some more and you can have some oatmeal porridge. And you, I don't know your name, but if you come with Tasha you must be all right. Here, sit. Or perhaps you would like to wash? The bathroom isn't large, but here is soap and hot water. The latch is here on the inside of the door.

She fairly pushed Ari inside and then turned back to Tasha. "Oh, my dear, dear Tasha. Is it really you? Your hair! Look at your hair! But of course, you had to cut it. Everyone knows of your beautiful hair. Look at how the color is so blotchy. Why, you have bleached it. Look how stiff it is. But that is good, too. It looks nothing like your beautiful hair. Oh how I loved to comb it. What a pity. Yes, the bleach is a very good idea, but you must do a better job. I can get some bleach from the apothecary. Old Wilhelm will give me some."

Ana turned to stir the porridge on the stove and added some salt. "Of course, I can't tell him it is for you. His shop may be watched. But he won't ask questions. I'll just tell him a friend wants to blend in her gray hairs. He'd never believe that I wanted it for me. These red curls aren't quite as dark as they were, but I'm not gray yet. Blackberry jam. That's what I'll do. He loves my blackberry jam. He'll give me some bleach for a jar of jam."

Ari emerged from the bathroom and stood staring in amazement at the tiny woman bustling around the room in front of him. Clearly he had never seen anyone like her in his life. Since her first sight of Tasha neither of them had been able to say a word. Tasha caught his eye and shrugged her shoulders, a half smile on her lips.

Looking up, Ana saw Ari standing there and immediately turned her attention on him. "Oh good, you are ready to eat. Come and sit down. Tasha, run along and wash up. I'm sorry, I don't know your name. But never mind. Don't tell me. It's better in these times that I don't know who you are. What fun. After you are gone I can tell all my friends I met a handsome mystery man. Oh, don't worry. But it's nice even for an old maid to have a man in her life once in a while. There, here is a nice bowl of porridge. I baked yesterday. Isn't it lucky that I thought to make sweet honey rolls. Here's a nice big one."

She brought a large pitcher to the table. "Look, there is milk too. Old Braun still has his cows. The 'good king' is even letting Young Braun take over the dairy. Old Braun likes strawberry jam the best. It's good I make plenty. He keeps me in milk. Jams and jellies are very good things to trade.

"Of course, I have to trade for everything. No one will hire me as a governess now. I might teach something subversive like all men are alike before God and no one is better than another, or that each man should work for his own living and not glut himself on the labors of others. But jams and jellies speak a universal language. Even royalists are not above eating mine, and they always make sure I get enough sugar to make them. They are the best in the country. I'm sorry, but I just can't say kingdom. The old democracy was too precious to me. And now to think I have seen my Tasha again, alive and well."

Ana finally paused and fumbled in her pocket for a handkerchief. Tasha emerged from the bathroom, walked over, and put her arms around Ana's slender shoulders. "Why, she's not even as tall as Gil," she thought.

"Oh, Ana, it's so good to see you. Is it safe for us to rest here?"

Ana opened her eyes wide. "You must not go anywhere else. You can't trust anyone. Many who once seemed so faithful to your father and said they loved him are the very ones who fawn at the feet of Com and his men of 'royal birth.' Royal birth! The kittens of my old Tabby cat have more royal blood in them than those simpering fools. Here, Tasha, eat. Oh how you hated good hot oatmeal porridge. I daresay it tastes good now. I skimmed some cream from the milk this morning. It will make the porridge into a feast. And the rolls. You must have a honey roll. And you, here, my mystery gentleman, eat another roll."

Ana rushed to serve him another of the giant rolls and filled his glass again with the creamy milk. "But we haven't all gone over to Com. Old Samuel can still be trusted, and Sally. She lets us know what is happening in the palace. Some people leave. Here one day, gone the next. Some are arrested, some go to join Marko. His forces are getting stronger. We sometimes hear things.

"Maple sugar," Ana continued. "I like to use it in my rolls, but it's hard to get now. I still have the honey from my bees and of course the jam. I hide the honey, though.

If they search and find it, they take it with them. But I can't blame the guards. I think they keep some for themselves. No one has enough of anything now."

"But Ana," Tasha interrupted. "What if they come and search your house again? Two sleeping wanted people are only going to get you killed."

"Oh, you can't sleep in the bed. I wish you could. Dear Tasha, I wish I could give you my house and all that's in it. I'll make places for you in the cellar. It is cool and a little dampish in the spring, but I have some straw ticks and lots of quilts. If you are as tired as you look, I daresay you'll sleep well. You won't mind the dampness?"

Tasha thought back to the long days and nights in the cold dampness and absolute darkness of the cave and laughed. "No, Ana. It will be like coming home to a palace."

The hot porridge laced with thick cream, tall glasses of cold milk, and fresh honey rolls were like a feast. While they ate Ana bustled around the room, her tongue as quick as her movements. As soon as they were finished she whisked the food out of sight, bundled up the tablecloth, and went outside to shake it.

To someone passing by, she was merely cleaning up after breakfast, but her quick eyes were searching the boundaries of her yard, looking for anyone who might be watching her house. She hung the tablecloth over the nearby clothesline, pulled open the long sloping cellar door, and stepped quickly down, emerging a minute later with a jar of jam in each hand.

After another searching look around the yard, Ana ducked back into the door and bustled Tasha and Ari outside and down the steps. She lit a small lamp and showed them a room with straw ticks on wooden bedsteads and quilts stacked neatly on shelves along the wall.

"Of course everyone has to have a place to go to if a tornado comes through," Ana said. "Not even the soldiers questioned my room down here. Take the lamp, Tasha. You'll have to make your own beds. I must get the door shut. If I stay here too long, someone may come down looking for me. There is a jug of water in the corner and dried fruit and meat in these other sealed jars. It's cool down here so they keep well if I can keep the mold from getting to them. I'll come back after dark. It won't be safe before then."

She handed the lamp to Tasha, gave her a quick hug and darted up the steps, closing the cellar door behind her. Too tired to even think, Tasha pulled a quilt from the shelf, took off her shoes, and lay down on the bed. Ari blew out the lamp, and Tasha shut her eyes against the quiet dusk of the basement room.

XIII

IN SPITE OF HER WEARINESS, TASHA AWOKE AFTER ONLY a few hours of sleep. She picked up her quilt from the bed and stood. Stepping carefully so as not to awaken Ari, she walked into the main storage room. A small window high in the west wall let in a little light. From the angle of the rays she could tell that it was early afternoon.

Tasha wrapped the quilt around herself and sat down on the steps, trying to think. Was it foolish for her to have insisted on coming? Would she really be able to help Ari get the papers he wanted? She wasn't even sure what they were looking for. And once the papers were stolen, what good would they do? If there were plans of attack or troop deployment, those plans would certainly be altered long before they would be able to get them into Marko's hands. There had to be something else, something more that Ari wanted. But what? And why hadn't he told her?

She stood up and started to pace the narrow room. How

did Ari know of the existence of the hidden compartment? He said he knew the old house well enough. Perhaps he had found out about it from Marko. When her father had abdicated the throne and established the democratic republic, Marko had been elected its first president. He knew of the compartment. All the really important state documents had been kept there, the letter of abdication, the new constitution...

The constitution! Was that what Ari was after? There had been many copies made at the time, but Com had destroyed as many as he could get his hands on. Would he destroy the original? The original had been placed in the compartment, and so had her father's letter. She remembered the night he had done it. He had made a little ceremony of it, placing it in the compartment, securing the lock, even having them practice opening the hidden door so that she and Marko would have access to it if they needed it, especially the letter.

So that she and Marko would have access to it. The three of them were the only ones in the room. Com wasn't there. Maybe her father hadn't trusted him with the knowledge of the compartment after all.

She sat down on a barrel and tried to think back. No, that wasn't right. Someone else was in the room that night. He stood well back in the shadows. She had assumed it was some kind of guard or servant. Father had read aloud his letter of abdication before placing it inside. In that letter all rights to the government were to be given to the people, and all descendants of his *father* were stripped of any rank or right to rule, except as they were elected by popular ballot. It wasn't just Tasha and her children, but any others descended from her grandfather who would lose their claim to the throne. But what other descendants were there? Her father's only brother was dead, and she knew of no descendants.

She remembered seeing her father pause to look at the stranger before he placed the document in the compartment. She had looked around then and saw the man nod in agreement. Then came the part when her father had made them practice opening the hidden door. When they turned to leave, the stranger had gone. Was Ari the stranger in the room that night? Why was he there? Why was it so important now that he retrieve those papers?

The sound of a jar breaking on the kitchen floor above startled Tasha. Since she had awakened she had heard Ana moving around in the rooms upstairs. Now there was more than Ana's quick step. Tasha could hear the thud of heavy boots. Someone must be searching the house once again.

Tasha grabbed the quilt and hurried into the other room. She stuffed her feet into her shoes. Ari had been awakened by the breaking glass and was up. There was a small storage room behind the sleeping room. Ari gave each of the straw ticks a brief shake to erase the impression of their bodies. He grabbed the lamp and set it on a high shelf and then followed Tasha into the smaller room.

There were large barrels stacked in the back corner, but Ana had left a space behind them large enough for them to hide in.

"Quick!" Ari commanded, "behind the barrels."

They could hear the cellar door being opened and the footsteps descending the stairs. Ana was keeping up her usual chatter, only this time she was sputtering just like someone who has been doused with cold water.

"Why do you always keep coming back? You never find anyone here but me. Why are you forever searching my house? Now look at the mess on my kitchen floor. To think of your just barging in like that, startling me. That jar of jam was the one I had made to take to tomorrow's fair. All that work wasted."

Now they were in the sleeping room. Ana's voice was triumphant. "There, you see, empty as it has always been. And you don't have to ruin two perfectly good ticks by ripping them with that knife. Have you no hands that you can feel the difference between straw and someone hidden? Now I shall have to spend an afternoon just mending ticks when I could have been doing something else."

There was a brief flash of light in the small storage room and then the footsteps receded, followed by Ana's strident voice. "You never make up your minds. First we are told to prepare places of shelter for ourselves and others in times of storm. Then you barge in and rip my nice straw ticks to shreds..."

There was a loud bang as Ana let the cellar door drop.

They could hear the sound of boots on the gravel walk and then all was quiet except for the steady sound of Ana's rocking chair on the floor above.

Tasha knew what Ana was doing. She had seen her do it countless times when something had happened to upset her. She would sit in her rocking chair, her body hunched over, her apron over her head, and she would rock and weep. When her tears were spent she would stand up, smooth her apron, wash her face, and go about her work as if nothing had happened.

Tasha's legs were numb before Ari finally rose, slipped from behind the barrels, and then reached back to help Tasha to her feet. The straw ticks in the other room had been slashed and the straw scattered. The room was nearly pitch black. Tasha gathered what straw she could by feel and stuffed it back into the mattress. Her fingers could make out several places where the tick had been mended. So this was not the first time the soldiers had used their knives to make work for Ana.

When she could find no more straw, she reached for the quilt and sat huddled on the bunk. Who knew if someone was still outside, listening and searching? If they were found it would mean certain punishment for Ana.

Finally the rocking above stopped and they heard the sound of glass being swept up, followed by the swish of a mop. There was a long period of silence and then at last they heard the cellar door open. Ana entered, feeling her way in the dark.

"Tasha? Oh, Tasha, you are still here. I didn't know but what you might have left. You must have found my spot behind the barrels. Come, quickly now. You must eat."

Ana led them up the steps and into the house. Then she went back outside to carefully secure the cellar door. Entering the kitchen once more she turned and threw the bolt before she lit a small lamp that was on the kitchen table.

"The shutters are closed, but we should move around as little as possible. I daresay you want to wash up before supper. Here, you, my mystery man, go on in. I have heated the water."

Ana's strength seemed to fail her and she sat down heavily. Tasha knelt beside her, her arm around Ana's shoulders.

"Oh, Ana, we should not have come here. We have put you into so much danger."

"No, Tasha, it was right for you to come. The searches, they will come no matter. It is a way of life for all of us now. They search for people, they search for gold, they search to instill fear into the people. They search to teach that no one is safe from them, not even in their own homes. You heard the breaking glass then? I did not know any other way to warn you. They always come so suddenly. Sometimes they enter the cellar first; this time they came first into the house."

Ana drew a handkerchief from her pocket and blew her nose fiercely. "If it weren't for Com, I don't know what would have happened to me."

Tasha stiffened. "Com? But he is the reason for all of your troubles."

"Oh, yes, Com's the one who orders the searches, but other than making a mess of my straw ticks, they know better than to damage things around here." She stood and pulled a pan of bread from the oven, upturning it on a white cloth.

"When the searches started, some of the soldiers took liberties. They used them as an excuse to take whatever they wanted. One made the mistake of carrying off my blue crock."

"Your cookie jar!" Tasha nearly laughed at the memory. Ana had spent long hours tutoring at the palace, but even during her time off, the children would not leave her alone. Her house by the river with its gardens and berry bushes was a magnet. And always there were cookies in the blue crock. It wasn't just Tasha and her girlfriends who lined up for treats from the crock. Com and the other boys did too, even Marko.

Ana turned over the loaf of bread and buttered the crisp top. "Of course it was full of cookies. He made the mistake of offering some to Com. He thought he'd be pleased. He was furious. Made the young man bring it back with an apology and a sack of flour as a gift. Then he let everyone know that anyone bothering anything of mine would be strictly disciplined." She wiped her hands on a towel. "Oh, the searchers come, especially since they have been looking for you. They rip my tick, and take a jar of honey if they find it, but even that would stop if I were to report them."

Ari emerged and Ana rushed around serving plates of greens seasoned with butter and vinegar, thin slices of meat fried crisp, new potatoes creamed with fresh green onions, thick slices of fresh bread, frosty glasses of milk, and, finally, large bowls of fruit soup made with all kinds of dried fruit, smothered in thick cream.

No one took the time to talk. Even Ana was silent until the meal was over. But as they washed the dishes Tasha asked, "Ana, when you were in the cellar with the soldiers, you said something about a fair tomorrow."

"Oh, yes, it is a great celebration, the anniversary of the coronation. There will be people coming from all over. People have already started to gather to see the grand procession. There will be games, dancing, and feasting. All free of course—paid for by the taxes Com has placed on us. But the people don't see it that way. Fools. They complain of the taxes, but lap up the handouts the taxes buy. I am sorry Tasha, but many of the festivities will be held in your old home. They say the king himself will join the dancing on the lawn. Many of the rooms will be open for tours."

"That's perfect." Tasha turned. "Ari, with all of that going on, it will be easy to get lost in the crowd."

Ana held up her hand. "Wait. Why you are here, I do not want to know." She quickly wiped out the sink and hung up her towel. "I will go to my room. There are quilts on the sofa in the living room. Tasha, whatever reason you had to come here, I don't care. I am just grateful you came to me and remembered your old teacher. Good-bye, my dear Tasha. I will be at the fair early in the morning. I will not know you if I see you."

She pulled two small bottles out of her pocket. "Here is the bleach for your hair. I had no trouble getting it from Old Wilhelm. He even gave me this shampoo for you to wash it out. He is glad for a jar of jam now and again. I'm sorry I cannot help you more." She gave Tasha a fierce hug. "Thank you for coming to me."

Blinded by tears, Ana rushed into her own bedroom and shut the door. Once again they heard the sound of the rocker, and finally the creak of springs as she climbed into bed.

"Come," Ari said at last. "We must not put Ana into any more danger. We will find a traveling caravan and camp with them the rest of the night. You are right. The festival is the perfect time to enter the city."

Tasha finally located their packs far back in one of the kitchen cupboards. They felt much heavier, and she opened them to find that Ana had packed each with carefully wrapped fresh rolls, fried meat, and small bunches of early radishes and green onions. Their water bottles had likewise been filled, and tied in a corner of a handkerchief in each pack was a small handful of coins. In the old days it would have been pocket change for Tasha, now it represented a good deal of work and saving for her old teacher.

Tasha felt the hot tears sting her eyelids as she repacked the bag. No, they could not stay, but someday they would return again. The injustices heaped on this one woman were multiplied again and again under the new regime. They must do all they could to hasten its downfall.

XIV

*T*HEY LEFT THE HOUSE AND FOLLOWED THE PATH to the footbridge, keeping to the shadows. After crossing the river they followed it north and west toward the main road and the large bridge that marked the entrance to the city. As they came in sight of what was now called the "King's Highway," they could see several campfires marking where festival travelers had stopped for the night.

Leaving Tasha in the shadow of some large bushes that grew along the banks of the river, Ari moved silently forward toward the camps. Tasha wrapped herself in a blanket and leaned against the packs. They still had not taken time to talk, and she had no idea what it was exactly that Ari was looking for.

She pulled the bottle of bleach from her pocket and started to comb it through her hair. Then, kneeling on a stone beside the river, she scooped some water into her hand. Lifting it toward her face, she was assaulted by its foul smell. Com and his band had managed to ruin even the beautiful river.

She used the water Ana had packed for her to wash and rinse her hair. She was drying it with a corner of the blanket when Ari returned.

"We are in luck. I have located a caravan of some very old and trustworthy friends. They are acrobats and magicians and have been invited to perform tomorrow in the great hall of your father's house."

Tasha bent and dipped her hand into the river. "Smell this, Ari. Is there nothing that Com does not pollute?"

Ari took her by the shoulders and turned her to face him. "That, my dear Tasha, is why we are here. The anger is there, but it must always be kept inside. Not a raging furnace that will soon burn itself out, but a steady glow that will give us strength for tomorrow and the day after, and the day after that. Now come. My friends are waiting."

They picked up their bundles and made their way around the edge of the camps toward the brightly painted wagon belonging to "Angelino and His Amazing Acrobats."

Suddenly a uniformed guard stepped out of the shadows, blocking their way.

"You, there. Curfew has been called. Why are you still wandering around the camp?"

Carelessly Ari draped his arm around Tasha's shoulders and drew her close.

"Camp's too crowded fer them what wants a little privacy. Don't you think?"

"And the bundles?"

"Come, the lady's not supposed to sit on cold ground and go without supper is she now?"

Ari drew out one of Ana's fragrant honey rolls. "Here now, we even have a bit left, if you'd like to share."

The guard glanced quickly around and then wrapped the roll in his handkerchief and tucked it in his pocket.

"Where is your camp?"

"Why, right over there. We're part of Angelino's crew. Here on special invitation of the king hisself. Come, join us."

There was a noticeable stiffening in the guard's spine. "I can only escort you to your camp. I must warn you not to leave your company again."

Ari gave him a friendly slap on the shoulder. "Of course. With you chaps around we'll likely be safe tonight."

He put his arm around Tasha's waist and hurried her over to the large campfire at the center of Angelino's camp. Once there he deposited her on a large log that had been rolled near the fire to make a seat.

"I must talk with Angelino. We need to plan for tomorrow. Wait here," he whispered before disappearing into the night.

Tasha groaned and sat hunched on the log. The warmth of the fire felt good, but its heat on her face was almost more than she could stand. She turned herself around, letting the blanket around her shoulders shield her from the heat while allowing a delicious warmth to penetrate her back.

The rich food Ana had given them coupled with the tension from being stopped by the guard had her stomach in turmoil. She felt like making herself retch, but knew she needed the strength the food would give her tomorrow.

A woman stepped down from the large wagon and walked to where Tasha was sitting. "Here, my dear. I thought you might like a cup of mint tea. Ari said you were stopped by a guard. This will help settle your nerves."

Tasha took the tea gratefully, and managed a wan smile of thanks. Just holding the cup of warm, fragrant liquid helped her relax. The woman sat down beside her.

"I am Vera. Angelino is my husband. You cannot be part of the act tomorrow. Ari says you have other things to do. But you must be listed on our roster to gain you entrance into the city. I have put you down as maid and cook."

She looked closely at Tasha's face. "I daresay you are more accustomed to having one than being one, but I don't know where else to put you, unless perhaps you can juggle?"

Tasha shook her head and sipped the tea. "Cook, I can do. Juggle I cannot. Thank you for your kindness."

"It is nothing. Ari is an old and very dear friend. He has helped us more than once. Most of what we have, we owe to him."

"Ari seems to have lots of old friends."

"Ah—yes. That is the kind of person Ari is. He will help and give, but never cross him. He will always remember. A good friend. A formidable enemy. You are lucky to be on the same side. Com underestimated him. He will regret it."

Vera rose and shook out her long skirts. "Ari will return soon. Do not worry about safety. My sons are keeping watch." She disappeared back into the wagon.

Tasha finished the tea. Vera was right. It did help to calm her nerves and settle her stomach. She looked around. Lounging around the little circle that was their camp were four tall young men. This one sitting on a rock, whittling; another casually leaning against the wagon; another coaxing a tune from a mouth organ; and the other juggling various objects. All were turned with their backs to the fire, their eyes searching the darkness beyond the flickering light.

In a moment, Vera emerged again from the wagon and sat down beside Tasha on the log.

"They need you inside. I will help keep watch out here."

She reached for a small log and threw it on the fire. Sparks flew upward and the young men turned and nodded and smiled at their mother. Tasha mounted the steps and opened the small door.

It was as if a cabin had been built in the wagon box. The walls and roof were of wood. A window, made of several small panes of glass, was covered with a bright orange curtain. A similar curtain closed off what must have been sleeping quarters in the back third of the little room. A small stove that could be used for both heating and cooking stood in one corner. Next to it was a sink, drained to the outside by a tube. On the other side was a table, surrounded by benches. Cupboards lined the walls, and pans, loops of sausages, and braids of garlic and onion hung from the ceiling. A strong smell of spice and herbs permeated the air and helped give the place a feeling of home.

A lamp with an orange shade was on the table, its wick turned down low. Angelino rose when Tasha entered.

"So, you are Susana," he said, bowing low. "A pleasure to have you with us." He smiled and Tasha noticed his teeth were even and very white under his mustache. "Good cooks are so hard to come by, and my wife can always use help with her costumes. But you have much to discuss, and I must care for the animals. Good night."

With that he was gone.

"Ari," Tasha's voice was insistent. "These people are wanderers. Can we trust them?"

Ari smiled. "I would not engage them in a game of chance unless I was prepared to lose everything I had. But"—his voice hardened—"I would trust them with my life, which is much more than I can say for those upstanding citizens who abandoned Marko as soon as Com smiled in their direction. The old ways are over, Tasha. You must now face the reality that those who wish only for comfort are not to be trusted."

Tasha shook her head. "Surely not all of them have sided with Com."

"Not all, but apart from a few who were left behind on purpose, most of those former leaders who truly support the democracy are across the river with Marko. It is the common people we depend on."

Tasha was sitting with her elbows propped on the table. Ari reached across and grabbed her wrist, squeezing it in his powerful grip.

"You will see many familiar faces tomorrow. You must acknowledge none of them." He shook her arm. "Do you understand? Trust no one."

He let her arm drop and Tasha rubbed at the red marks on her wrist.

"I understand. And am I now Susana?"

"Yes, I could not give even Angelino your real name. It would put his family in too much danger."

"Ari, why are we even here? What is it you are after?"

"Military papers will be most valuable. Those will be in the lockbox in the office downstairs. That will be my job. You must go upstairs to the bedroom in the west wing and open the hidden compartment. I do not think there is much there, but what there is is most vital. I don't think Com even knows of its existence. You know of your father's letter and the original of the constitution."

He withdrew a packet from inside his shirt. "These are copies. Take out the originals and replace them with the copies. You will also find one more thing inside. It will be in a white envelope like this one. This is the most important document of all. *You must remove that envelope and replace it with this one.* Do not fail me in this, Tasha."

She looked into his eyes. What was there? Anger, determination, yes, but also sorrow and profound hurt. An emotional fire, banked and controlled, but burning deep and strong. It was the steady glow he had told her about, pushing and sustaining him "tomorrow, and the next day, and the day after that."

He handed her a leather pouch threaded on a long thong, a small leather envelope inside of it. "Tie this bag around your waist. Put the envelopes into this smaller one, tie it shut, and then put it into the one at your waist. This tab from the small bag must be pulled to the outside."

She took the bags and fingered the soft leather. Ari continued, "Return as quickly as you can to the main hall. Angelino and his family will be there performing. Their act now calls for one of the boys to tumble down the hall, going so fast that he will enter into the crowd. You must work your way to the front row. After he tumbles away, you will no longer have to concern yourself more with the packet. It will be passed safely out of the house."

Tasha shook her head. "Thieves and pickpockets. Ari, how can you trust these people?"

"They are artists only of the sleight of hand. They are accused of much, but they steal nothing. As I said, do not ever hope to win if you are foolish enough to challenge them in a game of chance. But they have promised to help us, and we can trust them to fulfill that promise. They will give their own lives before they will let those papers fall into the wrong hands."

"And when is all of this to take place?"

"There is first the great ceremony and dancing on the green. Food tents will be set up, and those who will may gorge themselves throughout the day. Shortly after midday the festival will move inside the great house. When Angelino and his family start their show, that is when you must slip upstairs. There will be tours of the house. Perhaps you can join one of them. I would suggest that once you are upstairs you use the back hallway from the south dressing room to enter the west wing."

Tasha looked at Ari in amazement. How did he know of that hallway? He seemed to know every inch of the house. Had Marko told him all that? *"I know the house well enough,"* he had said. She started to ask him about it, then thought better of it. "He will tell me in his own time," she thought. Asking now might only cause more problems.

Instead she asked, "How much time will I have?"

"Close to half an hour. Don't delay too long. They are gifted performers, but they cannot go on forever. The tumbling act is part of their grand finale. They are here under royal command, but they do not want to stay any longer than they need to. They were very happy to know that in obeying the order of a despot, they might help strike a blow against him."

Ari leaned forward and took her hand, gently this time,

in both of his. "The military plans I will get are important. The papers you will replace are essential if we are to overthrow Com. *Do not fail me, Tasha.*"

"I will do my best," Tasha replied. "And if that is not enough"—she shrugged—"perhaps I will find that inside there is a part of me that can do more."

"That is all I ask." Ari's grip tightened and his voice grew husky. "Go with God."

Ari rose abruptly and went outside. After a long while, Tasha followed, found her blanket, and rolled up in it next to the fire. Three of the young men had gone to sleep. The other walked quietly around the campsite. Vera rose and entered the wagon. As she dozed off, Tasha was aware of the soft murmur of voices and quiet laughter as Ari and Angelino talked over old times.

XV

TASHA DRESSED CAREFULLY IN THE DRESS BEN HAD given her. It was much too large. Tasha couldn't help smiling. Instead of giving her one of Lora's dresses, which would have fit, he had given her one of his mother's. Her eyes burned, and Tasha blinked back the tears as she thought of Marta and Lora. They saw each other only once or twice a year, but Lora was her best friend as well as her cousin. People often mistook them for sisters, even though Lora's blond beauty was a striking contrast to Tasha's dark hair and eyes.

Marta and Tasha's mother had the same differences in their complexions, but their smiles, their mannerisms, even the sound of their voices were so alike everyone knew at once they were sisters. With the birth of many children and the life on a working farm, however, Marta was no longer the slender aunt from Tasha's childhood. The dress was much too big around.

Vera dug into the large supply of scarves that she kept for some of her acts and found a long, narrow one that contrasted nicely with Tasha's dress. Tasha tied the leather bag Ari had given her around her waist and then covered it with the scarf. The long ends hung over the bag, concealing it from view. She tied another scarf over her head, hiding all but the front part of her hair. She looked in the small mirror Vera had hung on the wall of her bedroom and was surprised at how old she looked in the loose dress, with only the bleached-out hair showing under the scarf.

Ari, too, had changed. His shock of white hair was hidden under a bandanna, and his skin, already tanned, was darkened further with makeup. He sported a thin, dark mustache, and in place of his brown leather tunic and brown shirt, he wore a blousy silk shirt of dull red. If possible, he would later exchange this shirt for one of the uniforms worn by the royal guard, but for now he looked as if he belonged to the acrobatic troop.

Angelino appeared in the doorway. "Come, we must all ride outside or walk. When we enter the city they will search the wagon and no one must be found inside."

He had already hitched up two large horses to the front of the wagon. Their white manes and long white tails contrasted with their brown coats, and their large hoofs were accented by a ruff of white hair as well.

The front seat was barely long enough to seat Angelino and Vera. Tasha was too nervous to sit and welcomed the chance to walk beside the wagon. Ari walked beside the horses, one hand resting on the broad withers of the horse next to him. The four young men also walked, one juggling some oranges, the others turning handsprings, leapfrogging over each other, and generally giving a nice preview of their coming show.

They passed a group of small children, their clothing ragged and hunger in their eyes. The juggler moved toward them, and when he had their full attention, he caught the oranges one by one and tossed them to the children.

"Well, at least they will get their stomach's filled at the festival," Tasha remarked to the young man.

"Not them," he said bitterly. "They are too poorly dressed. Only after the well-dressed adults have had their fill will the poor be allowed to eat any leftovers, and the poor children will eat last of all. There won't be much left for them."

They had started early, so the delay at the bridge was not long. The guards were very thorough, however, and before they finished with Angelino's wagon, the line behind them reached back nearly half a mile. Angelino had done his work on the documents well. The guards gave Ari and Tasha only a brief look before searching the wagon. Finally, the guards waved them on, and Angelino urged the horses forward. They were glad to be moving again and stepped out with a briskness Tasha did not think they possessed.

Inside the city, Angelino pulled off on a quiet side street and stopped the wagon.

"We must separate now. We will look for you at the end of our performance." He shook Ari's hand. "Do not worry, old friend, a magician's wagon has many hiding places. Our next scheduled performance will be in Elmore."

He gave the reins a shake, and the big horses moved off.

"It will be better if we are not seen together," Ari said. "I will wait for you under the footbridge that leads to Ana's house. I have already hidden our packs there.

"Here." He thrust the handkerchief and coins Ana had given her into her hand. "You may need the money. Meet me at dusk." He turned and walked back down the street the way they had come, vanishing into an alley.

Tasha put the handkerchief and coins into her pocket, then turned and looked around her. This was the part of town where the craftsmen had lived when her father was alive. Though it remained much the same, there were small differences. Weeds grew up around the street sign. A broken window in one house had not been replaced, but covered with a piece of wood. Paint was starting to peel from the shutters of another house. A cat, thin and dirty, sat in the morning sunshine on a stoop and attempted to groom itself.

In spite of the warmth of the late spring sunshine, Tasha shivered, as she walked down the familiar streets. She wished she had asked Vera for one of her shawls.

The crowd was already gathered on the sward in front of the great house. Tasha was not prepared for the burning pain she felt as she rounded the corner and caught sight of the home of her childhood. How many happy memories were there! A child with long dark curls skipped by, laughing and holding her father's hand. Tasha turned away, hot tears burning in her eyes.

"Oh, Father," she thought, "if only you had lived. All this would not have happened."

Struggling to compose herself, she leaned back against the wall of a house. She felt a small tug on the scarf around her waist. A tiny girl, probably not much younger than Raina, stood there, fingering the soft silk. Tasha gasped and felt for the leather bag. The documents she needed to switch were still there. The child, her dirty face full of fear, fled into the alley.

Tasha straightened her shoulders. Her father was not alive, but she was, and so were Marko, Ari, Raina, the frightened little girl, her friends at the compound, and all the good people who had helped them.

Wiping the tears from her eyes with the back of her hand, she joined the crowd milling and moving toward the tall flagpole where a temporary stage had been set up. A chill ran down her spine and her throat tightened as she looked at the stage. It was identical to the one her father had set up the day he had publicly given up the throne and presided over Marko's inauguration as the first president chosen by the people.

Although Marko was only in his early twenties, no one who saw him raise his hand to the square that day doubted his ability to govern wisely and well. Her father had been overjoyed that the people had ratified his own choice of a successor from those he had so carefully trained.

A large chair with carved armrests and a velvet upholstered seat stood on the ground between the flagpole and the stage. This was obviously for "King Comnor." He had thrown his cloak carelessly over the back of the chair and it trailed on the ground. Then she saw him.

Comnor stood a little in front of the chair, ready to mount the stage. A bevy of young girls surrounded him, openly flirting with him. He looked up and his eyes surveyed the crowd. Tasha shrank behind a large woman holding up a wiggling toddler. His eyes had seemed to pause. Had he seen her? One of the girls tugged at Com's sleeve, and, laughing, he looked down at her, gave her a kiss full on the mouth, and then leaped onto the stage.

The girls followed him, took their place behind him, and started to sing. It must have been a new national anthem because the audience quieted as soldiers raised a large flag. The background colors were the same as the old flag, but the constellation pointing to the Unchanging Star had been replaced with a large crown, superimposed upon crossed swords.

"How appropriate," Tasha thought. "The sword and the crown replacing man's free will under God."

Apparently this was the great unveiling of the new national symbol. Com started into a long speech, explaining, justifying, excusing the brutal actions of the past two years.

Most of the crowd stood and listened to their king, especially those who courted his favor. But many on the edges found it hard to hear, and drifted toward the great tables loaded with food. The smell of food made Tasha realize that she had not yet eaten and she too moved toward the tables.

There were mounds of oranges, apples, plates of candied squash, bowls of stewed rhubarb, platters of crisp bacon and ham, and great plates piled high with deep-fried bread scones.

Tasha selected a hot scone and was pleased when the serving woman also gave her a small paper cup of honey to pour on it. As Com droned on, she found herself wandering toward the ornate chair. The crowd had moved in, filling the space between the stage and the chair. As she passed behind the chair she stumbled, nearly dropping her bread and honey.

The ground, which from a distance looked like a smooth carpet of grass, was in reality, rough and uneven. Gopher tunnels, clumps of thistles, and even anthills, marred the once-perfect lawn.

Anthills! Tasha paused. There was one not far from the chair. If Com hated anything it was insects—cockroaches, ants, grasshoppers, even butterflies.

Tasha glanced around. Everyone seemed intent on Com's address. Carefully she tipped her small cup. A drizzle of honey ran down the velvet cloak from the high collar to the border. A small kick and the corner, left so carelessly on the ground by its owner, reached to the edge of a large anthill. Another drizzle of honey, and then another small kick to the hill itself to set the ants swarming. Tasha moved around to the fringe of the crowd behind the stage and finished her bread and what was left of the honey. It was delicious.

XVI

Tasha wandered around the grounds, at once wanting to see a familiar face and at the same time fearful that she would and that he or she would recognize and betray her. On the side opposite the food tables, there was space set up for craftsmen to display their wares. She walked up to Ana's table and stood, admiring the shimmering jars of jelly and the thick jams.

"A beautiful day for a festival," she said.

"Oh, yes. A beautiful day. I daresay that is why we have such a large crowd. Haven't had so many people in one place for years." Ana looked nervously about.

Tasha pulled out the handkerchief Ana had given her and untied the corner. "Your jams and jellies are beautiful. Do you have some black raspberry?"

"Black raspberry? Of course. And from this past season, too. Everything was made just this past summer. No, no, one copper is plenty. Please, one is all I can charge for that jar. It is so small."

Tasha took back the coins she had tried to press into Ana's hand. They had been given as a gift and it would only embarrass and distress Ana if she did not keep them. "I'm sure one copper could never be enough for all the work that went into this. But thank you. Your generosity will be the sweetest memory of this day."

She could not keep up the charade any longer and turned away abruptly, trying to swallow the lump in her throat. Mentally she kicked herself. She should never have attempted to talk again to Ana. But she could not help herself. She needed someone to know that she had been there. That she had returned to stand in front of her father's house.

She glanced quickly back through the crowd. Ana was talking with another customer, but still daubing at the corner of her eyes with a spotless handkerchief. The jam was thick and rich and full of fruit. A passerby stopped and asked where she had bought it. She was glad to point out Ana's table, and hoped that the richly dressed woman would be asked to pay much more than one copper for a similar jar.

A group of folk dancers was now performing on the temporary stage. Com had stepped down and was seated in the large chair. A breeze sprang up, chilling the late spring morning, and through a break in the crowds, Tasha saw him draw his cloak around his shoulders.

A display of children's clothing caught Tasha's eye and she stopped to admire a vivid blue dress. Raina would look so pretty in it. She looked up at the woman standing behind the table, intending to ask her the price. The woman was staring at her through half-closed eyes, as if she were trying to place her. Instantly Tasha realized her mistake. This woman had been her own dressmaker before the war. Another customer stepped forward, and Tasha quickly turned away, hoping that she had not been recognized.

The folk dancers finished their number and a choir of children were taking their places on the stage. Tasha glanced at the sun. It couldn't be more than midmorning. The more she wandered around, the greater her chance of being recognized by someone. But if she were to just stand still, someone might become suspicious and investigate further.

Finally she saw a small food stand with a group of tables, set off on the side, where festival goers could sit and relax for a while. She made her way to a little table set back close to some shrubbery and requested a glass of lemonade. A large group came soon after and took the other two chairs from her table and moved them to one situated near the front. Tasha was relieved. Now she wouldn't have to make an excuse if someone came and wanted to share her table.

There was a disturbance over near the stage. She recognized Com's voice yelling, and through the crowd there was a flash of blue velvet. Tasha ducked her head and smiled. The ants had found their mark.

Finally she noticed that people were starting to move toward the big house. Tasha took her place in the moving crowd, trying not to meet anyone's eye, hoping that no one would notice her or recognize who she was. She could feel her heart pounding, and the lump in her throat made it hard to breathe as she walked once more over the worn flagstones, up the steps, through the gracious portico, and into the spacious entry hall.

This is where Angelino and his family would be performing. Some elderly ladies and gentlemen were already taking their places in some seats reserved for them. A chair, identical to the one outside, stood on a platform opposite the door. Com had not yet arrived.

Tasha saw Vera enter from the back. She walked up to her through the press of spectators, and handed her the jar. "Here is the jam you wanted for tonight's supper."

Vera was surprised, but took it in stride. Motioning to one of her sons, she handed him the jar to take to the wagon as Tasha merged back into the audience.

A group was forming to tour the house and Tasha joined them, staying to the back of the group and behind a tall, thin man dressed in the clothing of a farmer. His stout wife was beside him, and together Tasha hoped they would shield her from the guide, a middle-aged man who had worked for her father.

Behind her she could hear laughter and snatches of conversation. "Marko...border attack...on the run again... killed..." More laughter and then..."Probably got the president himself this time...won't stay behind...noble leader..."

The speakers drifted off, not following along on the tour. Tasha felt an ache in her hands and found that her fists were clenched so tightly her nails were digging into her palms. Had Marko been injured? Was he still alive?

She took a deep breath and forced herself to relax. Worrying would do no good. She had a job to do, just as Marko had his. She must not fail.

The group moved slowly through the house. As they passed the office door, Tasha quickly averted her eyes from the guard standing there. So, Ari had been able to find a uniform. If he saw her go by in the group he gave no indication, but she did not expect him to. At least they were both inside.

Upstairs, it was not hard to slip into the dark hallway leading to the master suite and what had been Marta and Lora's dressing room during their extended visits. Tasha found her way easily toward the master suite in the west wing. The tour would not be going down that way. She had looked down the main hall and seen a velvet cord draped across the entry, and a guard directing people down the stairs.

Anger choked her as she thought of Comnor possessing the rooms of her parents. She nearly burst into the room, wanting only to get everything over with so she could leave. She caught herself just in time, and stopped, noticing that the door was slightly ajar. Com was in the room.

He had apparently gone to change before the program. Would he be leaving by this hallway? There was a storage closet in the end of the hall. Tasha slipped inside and pulled the door shut.

The door to the room banged open. Tasha heard voices—Com angry, someone else, a quiet murmur. The voices faded away and the door shut with a soft click. Tasha waited, forcing herself to count to one hundred slowly. Had the person who closed the door walked away or was he waiting in the hall? Even worse, was he still inside the room?

She opened the door of the closet and looked out. The hall was empty. In the light from the dressing room at the other end she caught a glimpse of a liveried servant hurrying toward the sound of applause and cheers as Angelino and his family started their program.

The door to the bedroom opened silently. It had not been locked. Only someone who had lived here would know about the back hall and this door. She breathed a sigh of relief as she saw that the room was empty. There was a slight film of dust along the baseboard near the panel. If the panel had been moved since that long ago night, it had not been recently.

With only slight pressure, the carved wood moved aside, revealing another panel, even more intricately carved. With trembling fingers she counted the squares in the pattern— two down, three across on one side, six down, two across on the other. Releasing the small latch on each square, she gave a tug and the little wooden door swung open.

As Ari had said, there wasn't much in the hidden compartment, just the three envelopes and a small wrapped parcel about the same size and shape. Whatever the parcel contained Tasha did not know, but it did not belong to Com. She removed all four items and replaced them with those Ari had given her. The small leather bag was only big enough for the envelopes. The packet she tucked into the pocket of her dress. Placing the envelopes inside the compartment, she swung the door closed and slid the outer panel back in place.

She glanced around the room and started toward the door, then stopped. A short shelf had been built into the wall above the bed. Her father had used it to hold copies of his most beloved books. Now the books were gone. In their place was a heavy gold crown, encrusted with jewels. It was the emerald that stopped her. Her mother's emerald, still surrounded by small sparkling diamonds. The jeweler had only removed the bail from the crown holding the gems and had set the entire arrangement into the center of the crown.

She remembered the day her father had given the necklace to her mother. It had seemed a very ordinary day to Tasha, full of studies and sewing under Ana's watchful eye. Then there were her regular chores of helping the cook prepare supper. But as they sat down around the table, Father pulled a packet from inside his tunic and handed it to Mother with a pleased smile.

Tasha remembered the moment vividly. Not just because of the necklace, which caused them all to gasp at its beauty, but more because of what passed between her mother and father. There was a look, a communion of two souls, a feeling of love so strong that even as a child, Tasha felt she could reach out and touch it. And then they looked at her and drew her into their circle, their private union. Their love washed over her and held her.

There was a faint echo of cheers from below. Tasha tore herself away and hurried out the door. The papers must be delivered, but Com could not use her mother's emerald in such a way.

It didn't take her long to negotiate the passage and make her way down the stairs to the great hall. The crowd was large enough that many were watching from the stairs at either end of the hallway. Through the crowd she could see Angelino and his boys moving the crowd back to make more room for their finale. Ari was near the front, still dressed as a guard. Angelino himself was moving the crowd back in that part of the hall. Ari, seemingly distracted by something on the other end of the hallway, did not move back with the crowd. Angelino walked up to him, caught his attention, and gently pushed him back. Tasha knew that then, whatever papers Ari had found, they were now in Angelino's possession.

As best she could, without attracting too much attention, Tasha pushed herself toward the front of the crowd. The boys were tumbling now, somersaulting over their parents, who were standing back-to-back in the center of the cleared space. Faster and faster they tumbled, their forms just a blur of color passing each other, forward and back, crossing and re-crossing the hallway. Then the youngest boy came down the hall toward Tasha. He was going too fast to stop and the crowd instinctively moved back, leaving Tasha in the front. He knocked into her, causing her to stumble backwards. Instantly he was up, helping her gain her balance, speaking a quick apology, and then he was off again. There had been a brief smile, a flash of white teeth. She could smell his sweat and see the beads of it on his forehead. She did not need to touch the bag to know that the packet holding the envelopes was gone.

The boy tumbled back, still in time to make his final leap to the top of the pyramid his father and brothers had made. Vera was in front, taking the bows, leading the audience in their applause. Tasha melted back into the crowd. While things were still in confusion she had to return to the upstairs room.

Once again she made it into the large bedroom without incident. Taking the crown from its place, she then took out the knife Ari had given her in the cave. She had carried it with her ever since. The knife was tempered steel and the point was sharp. The large crown was soft gold and easily gave up the jeweled setting. She dropped the gems into the inside of her high-topped shoe and worked it down under her arch. It was uncomfortable, but less likely to be found if she were searched.

She replaced the crown, turning its face toward the wall, hoping to delay the time when the theft would be noticed, and walked quickly to the door and out into the hallway.

She was at the end of the hall, passing the dressing room door, when a shadow filled the doorway in front of her. Tasha looked up; there was no time to turn and hide. Com, surrounded by guards, stood looking down at her.

XVII

COM SMILED, BARING HIS TEETH. HE REMINDED TASHA OF a dog about to attack. Reaching forward with one hand, he pulled off the scarf that covered her hair.

"Well," he said, fingering the stiff locks, "I see that life on the run has not agreed with you, Tasha, my dear."

"Or"—his hand closed into a fist, pulling her hair—"perhaps you did this to yourself." She cringed, tears smarting her eyes. "A useless sacrifice, especially if you insist on coming into the heart of the Capital. What *are* you doing here? Have you changed your mind? Did you realize how much you really missed me?"

His hand released her hair and caressed her cheek. She slapped it away. "I would rather see a pack of fighting dogs than ever lay eyes on you again, Com."

"Then why are you here, in *my* house?" He reached out again and lifted her chin, forcing her to look into his eyes. "This is my house now, not yours. Not ever. Unless..."

She turned her head and knocked his hand away, then turned back and met his gaze. "Unless nothing, Com. I will never live in this house with you."

"Then you will never live here. Marko is gone. He has abandoned you and his people. He will never return." He reached out again to touch her hair.

"Keep your hands off me, Com. I am not one of your simpering social climbers. Enjoy living here while you can. Marko rules by the voice of the people. No matter what you assume, or what lies you speak, you will never be anything but an upstart. A poor boy who fancies himself a king."

"Oh, my dear, that is where you are very wrong. I long ago gave your father the documents proving my right to the throne. You look surprised. Don't be. He no doubt put them away, thinking they would not be needed. After all, you would become my wife and we would rule together."

He took her shoulders and pushed her backwards onto a bench in the small dressing room, motioning his guards to take their places behind and on each side of her. Then he too sat, on another small bench, crossing his legs and smiling in a way that many a foolish girl thought charming.

His voice became bitter. "Then Marko came with his wild ideas of rule by the masses. He brainwashed your father into giving up the throne."

He leaned forward then. "The throne, Tasha. *My* throne."

Tasha felt the anger lifting her out of her seat. The guards grabbed her arms, restraining her. "Marko did nothing of the sort. Father worked most of his life to get the people to the point where he could step down and turn over the reins of government. Why do you think you and all those other boys and girls were brought here for school? What was the purpose of all those exercises in the functions of government? He was only waiting, teaching, and looking until the people were prepared and someone was found who could be trusted with such an undertaking."

She sat back down and shook herself loose from the grasp of the guards. "And that someone wasn't you, Com. It was Marko. You failed every important test. Enjoy your time in the sun. It won't last."

Com raised his eyebrows. "Won't it, now? It will last. The documents I gave your father prove my right to the throne. You are a traitor and a deserter. I rule by right of birth, as son of your father's brother."

Tasha gasped. "But he had no children. He has been dead for years."

"He is dead, yes. But not childless. So your father never told you? He never showed you those papers?"

"If that had been true, my father would have told me. You are lying, Com."

"It is not a lie, and your father had the papers to prove it."

"Then show them to me." Tasha paused. "Wait." She continued slowly. "You say my *father* had those papers. You don't know where they are, do you, Com? Your proof is nowhere to be found. Your lie is nothing but that—a lie."

Com was on his feet. His hand shot out and slapped Tasha across the mouth, knocking her to the floor. "It is not a lie, and I have the proof. It is good you came back, Tasha. You can help me find those documents. Your father has placed them somewhere. I haven't yet found out where. But you will. You will find them or you will not live."

"Never, Com. I will never even attempt to look for anything that will help you."

"You will change your mind in time. Take her to the dungeon."

"Com..."

"Starting to change your mind already?"

"Never!"

"Then my guards will escort you. Perhaps after a few days in darkness, you will begin to see things differently."

Com started to leave and then turned, almost as an afterthought. "Oh, you know the many cats your father used to keep to make sure that rats and mice were never able to invade the old dungeon? I'm afraid they were all poisoned, somehow. Too bad. I hear the rats have started to come in."

Tasha looked hard at Com, noticing for the first time the mass of red welts on his neck and cheek. "Rats are appropriate for the house of Com. And insects too, I see. You keep no better company now than you used to. Rats and insects. They must recognize you as a brother."

"So, it was your hand that dipped into the honey pot."

133

He grabbed her wrist and twisted her arm behind her back. "You shouldn't have done that, Tasha. Your royal airs will not help you now."

He flung her to the floor. "There is one way you can come back, Tasha, only one. Refuse that and you will rot below ground. And you will still help me find those papers."

He turned on his heel and walked down the hall to the bedroom. Tasha, her arms held in the grip of the guards, was escorted down the back stairs, through the main floor kitchen, down into the basement, and on down into the old dungeon.

Built by some great-great ancestor, it was so long unused that most people did not know it even existed. Tasha knew, and Lora and Com. As the door slammed shut Tasha stood in the middle of the floor. It was chilly and she rubbed her arms for warmth. She knew the walls were covered with slime, and so was the floor. There was a scurrying sound, and she retched, thinking of the filth of their excrement under her feet.

Suddenly Tasha felt like laughing wildly at the absurdity of it all. Com would probably not have even known about the dungeon if it hadn't been for her and Lora. They had been about ten. It was a rainy day, and they spent it exploring the house, finding twisting hallways and unused stairs and passages, some which seemed to lead to nowhere. Through the years additions had been added on to additions, often with no overall plan or reason. Just "My lady wants a sunroom," or "My lord desires a conservatory."

A door in the basement pantry led down into the dungeon. It was their most exciting discovery of the day, and it was much too good to keep secret. Com had recently come with his mother to live in the house and study with the other boys and girls. He was older, but awkward and unsure, and he took out his frustrations by teasing the two girls.

The day before, he had taken Lora's new white kitten and tied its leg to a chair. Then he took a pan and wooden spoon and kept banging them together behind the little animal until it was frantic. The noise had attracted the girls, and Com had been led off in disgrace by his teacher. But that wasn't enough for the two girls. Com needed to be taught a lesson.

With promises of a surprise at the end, they had talked him into letting them blindfold him, and then led him into the dungeon. At the bottom of the steps, he had run into a spider web. That was enough for Com. He ripped off the blindfold, pushed the girls to the floor, and ran up the steps.

At first the girls sat on the bottom step convulsed in giggles. Then, when they mounted the stairs to leave, they realized Com had not only fled, he had locked them in. They huddled together in the darkness and held each other until they finally cried themselves to sleep. It was several hours later, when Tasha's father was about to mount a massive search for them, that Com confessed and the girls were released.

After that, Com had used Tasha's fear of the place to make her give him extra sweets and sometimes even her pocket money. After he grew older, he seemed to want to make amends and be her friend. But though she left behind her fear, she never trusted him, in spite of all his courtly ways and smooth tongue.

Then Marko arrived. Marko's jokes were funny but never mean. Even after being admitted into her father's school, he would go late to the barn and help Old Samuel with the chores. Tasha was assigned to take care of Raina, but Marko would show up whenever he could and take her and care for her himself. Raina openly adored her big brother, and Tasha found herself doing things she thought might please him.

Tasha couldn't tell how long she had been standing there in the middle of the little room. Her legs were numb and tired, but the thought of sitting on the cold filthy stone repulsed her so much she could not bring herself to do it.

Finally the door at the top of the stairs opened a crack and someone, holding a small candle, shuffled down the slippery steps, feeling his way. When he was close enough so that she could see his face, Tasha gasped. It was Old Samuel, her father's chief overseer and craftsman.

"Samuel," she said, embracing his stooped form. "You are still alive."

"Oh, yes, Miss Tasha, I just stay in the background and Com doesn't bother me much."

Tasha started to speak, but the old man held up his hand for silence.

"No time to talk. Here's a small candle and a few matches. It isn't much, but it'll keep the dark away for a little while. That may be all we'll need."

"Need? For what? Com will never let me leave."

"Shush," his voice was stern. "Are you traveling alone?"

"No, a man called Ari brought me."

"Ari, I thought as much. Where is he?"

"I was to meet him at dusk under the footbridge near Ana's house."

"Good. Good-bye, Miss Tasha." He started up the steps, feeling his way now without the candle. "It doesn't take a guard long to eat even a very large piece of pie. Old Sally is still in the kitchen. She's the one who saw you and told." He paused at the top of the short flight of steps. "We haven't all gone over to Com. We'll be waiting."

Again the door opened a crack, and the old man vanished. There was only the echo of the bolt being thrown on the other side, locking her in again.

XVIII

THE SMALL CANDLE HELPED. TASHA FORCED HERSELF to look at its cheerful flame and not at the glittering eyes and scurrying bodies of the rats and mice that it revealed. She climbed up and sat in the middle of the short stone staircase. Cupping her hands around the flickering light gave her a measure of warmth.

Samuel must be planning to contact Ari and arrange for her escape. How had he ever been able to enter in the first place and give her the candle? The penalty for a guard leaving his post for a piece of pie would surely be great if it were discovered. Could there be some, even in the ranks of the guards themselves, who had not gone completely over to Com?

She shifted her weight and felt the gem in her shoe. She should get rid of it in case she was searched. With the light of the candle she could see that the mortar around the old stones was crumbling. In the debris scattered about the floor she found a flat piece of rusty metal. She chose a stone in the wall next to the second step from the bottom. The rock wasn't large; it looked as though it had been put in more to fill a hole than as a real part of the wall.

She pulled out the stone. Behind it was nothing but damp earth, and it was easy to dig a small hole. Tasha ripped a length off her sash, wrapped the jewels, and put them into the opening, sealing it with the rock. Even if she herself wasn't able to retrieve it, someone else could, and the jewels would at least be out of Com's possession.

He would no doubt search the dungeon, but perhaps, before he found it, Old Samuel, or even Sally, could remove it and hide it again.

She heard the scrape of the bolt and quickly pinched out the flame, hoping that the thin smell of smoke would not be noticed in the musty air. As the door swung back she could hear voices, but she sat still, her head on her knees, the candle stuffed quickly into the corner between the step and the wall. A shaft of light illuminated the stairs and sent the rats scurrying.

"Oh, she's here, all right, sir. No way to get out of this place."

Footsteps descended the steps, stopping right behind her. It was Com's voice which spoke: "So, my dear Tasha, have you had enough? How beautiful the spring evening was. Stars in the sky, a perfect crescent of a moon. How lovely to walk in the open air between the rows of apple trees in blossom. I saw many of your friends, Jennete, Myra,

Donell. What a delightful time one can have, talking over old times."

Tasha didn't bother to answer. It was the same Com of old, only this time it wasn't a kitten tied to a table leg that he was tormenting, but Tasha herself. She thought of Ana, of Old Samuel, and of Sally in the kitchen. *We haven't all gone over to Com,* he had said. How many more were there? And how many were like Amoz, appearing to side with the royalists but supporting Marko's forces in whatever ways they could?

"Are you listening to me, Tasha?" Com's voice, louder now, interrupted her thoughts. "Things will not get better down here. And don't think you will be able to get out. I hear Old Samuel has been bumbling and shuffling around."

Tasha felt herself stiffen involuntarily. Com went on. "Poor old man, he could get hurt, out after dark the way he was. I had a soldier escort him home and gave instructions that he was to be watched day and night. I'm sure you appreciate my concern, don't you Tasha?" He nudged her back with the toe of his boot.

She heard his feet turn and mount the steps. There was a pause. "Oh, I'm sorry we could not invite you to the banquet tonight. The roast pork was most delectable. Your old governess, Ana, contributed some delicious jams and jellies. A pity. Not one crumb left. Donated to the poor. A commendable cause, don't you think? Enjoy your evening, Tasha. Sleep well."

The heavy door slammed closed and for the third time she heard the scrape of the bolt in the lock.

Tasha felt for the candle and found her fingers shaking. Part of the end was gone. In that brief time, even with the light on the stairs, a rat had started to eat it. What would they do to her if she fell asleep?

But even with that there was a bigger problem. What about Old Samuel? Did they suspect that he had managed to see her? If they did, what would happen to him? Would he also end up down here? It was unthinkable that someone who had served so long and done so much would have to suffer like that. But Com didn't care what happened to others, just so his own desires were fulfilled.

Then there was Ari. Had Samuel been stopped before he reached Ari and gave him the message about where she was? He must have been. Samuel had not been gone long enough before Com came. How long would Ari wait? He had what he wanted. The papers had been switched and were on their way to Elmore. Would he risk more to try to get her out? The compound was isolated with few guards, and Ari was familiar with the area and at home in the woods. How would he do in a city?

In leaving the compound, the signal had been sent. The White Dove had flown and Marko would soon return. How important was it to the cause that she actually join his forces on the other side of the river? How much would Ari—or even Marco—care if she came?

At the thought of Marko there was a sickness in the pit of her stomach. She remembered the snatches of conversation she had heard in the house. "Killed... probably got the president himself this time..." Someone, maybe many, had been killed in an attack. Marko had been there. Was he among the injured, or the dead?

She shivered and hugged her knees to her chest. Up the short flight of stairs, beyond the locked door, was her home—her bedroom with its feather bed, warm quilts, and lavender-scented sheets. Her old friends had spent the evening walking among the flower beds her mother had laid out and planted.

Then Ari's words in Angelino's wagon came back to her, *The old ways are over... those who wish only for comfort are not to be trusted.* She thought of the little girl she had seen that morning, of Josie and the others still in the compound because they had nowhere else to go, and of Ana, and Samuel and Sally. Whatever happened, she couldn't turn back.

She held the bit of candle in her hands. She would not light it yet. The darkness was not that bad. It was more comfort to know that the candle was there, waiting. Finally, exhausted, she slumped against the cold wall and slept. In her weariness she did not feel the tug of the rats, nibbling on the hem of her skirt.

Tasha was awakened by the throwing of the bolt. She barely had time to conceal the candle in the back of the step before the door banged open.

"Where is it, Tasha?" Com's voice was harsh. "What have you done with the emerald?"

Tasha sat unmoving, her head on her knees, her hands clasped around her legs.

"Guards! Bring that girl up here. She will learn not to defy me!"

Strong hands grasped Tasha and pulled her backwards up the steps, then dropped her onto the floor of the basement pantry.

Com stood over her, holding the crown, the mark on the front evidence of her tampering.

"Where is the emerald, Tasha?"

She pushed herself to her feet. She would not speak to Com from the position of an underling. "That stone never belonged to you, Com. It was a personal possession of my mother. Even your far-fetched claim for government cannot extend to private property that never belonged to the state."

"When Marko betrayed and deserted his country, I became its rightful ruler. This house and everything in it became property of the state. Your right of possession ended the day I assumed the throne. That jewel belongs to me, Tasha. Give it back and I may forget that you are not only a traitor, but also a common thief."

"That emerald is not yours, Com, and I will never give it back."

"Search her."

"But sir"—the guard was aghast—"this is my lady, Tasha."

"This girl is a thief. If you must, then call the housekeeper. She is to be searched."

Com turned on his heel and strode from the room.

The housekeeper came and took her into a private bathroom on the main floor. She was not new. She had been there for years and though she worked for Com, she treated Tasha with the utmost respect.

"I'm afraid you'll have to hand me all your clothes, Lady Tasha. I have another dress that you're supposed to put on. There's a screen. Just use it to change behind. The water in the basin isn't really warm, but the soap is good quality. I daresay you need to refresh and relieve yourself. Here's a glass of water to drink, too. Old Sally didn't think as you'd had anything to eat or drink."

"Thank you." Tasha drank the water gratefully, then quickly shed the dress and put the other one on. She noticed with delight that it was one of her own that she had once used to work in.

"Lady Tasha," the housekeeper's face was creased with concern. "This packet was in your pocket. It's not the emerald, is it?"

Tasha paused in her washing. She had forgotten about the packet she had removed from the compartment. "No, it is not the emerald. Just a keepsake that belonged to my father. Com cannot know of its existence, so he will not miss it. Please, don't give it into his hands."

"I have to serve Com. He's the king here, but I'm looking for an emerald, and this isn't it." She opened a cupboard and slipped the packet into a corner. "When you return, Lady Tasha, I'll have it waiting for you."

They went out into the hall where Com was waiting for them.

"Well?"

"Here's her clothes, every one of them, and I didn't see any emeralds."

"Guard, return this thief to the dungeon. She is to remain there without food or water until she gives back the emerald, or her flesh rots from her bones and she is eaten by the rats. Is that clear?"

"Yes, sir. Come, my lady."

Tasha left the room, her head high. She smiled at Com as she passed. His face clouded with fury.

XIX

THE DOOR SLAMMED SHUT BEHIND HER, AND ONCE more Tasha heard the grate of the bolt in the lock. Feeling her way in the darkness, she descended the steps to where she had hidden the candle. There was a scurrying sound and she felt for the stub with her foot. She touched a soft furry body and lashed out, nearly losing her balance. There was a thud as the animal hit the floor below. Reaching down, she found a bit of the candle and the few matches still intact.

Once more she sat on the steps, holding the candle in her hand. The kindness of the housekeeper, added to that of the others, brightened and warmed the dank cell.

Her new dress was much warmer and she was grateful. It was fine-spun wool, soft to the touch. The long sleeves hugged her arms and the full skirt protected her legs from the dampness. She tucked the candle into her lap and rested her head on her knees, her hands in the folds of the skirt. Once more she slept. It was easier than trying to stay awake, watching and wondering.

How long she stayed there, she had no way of knowing. Then suddenly the door above her swung open, footsteps descended and someone took her arm, lifting her to her feet. It was Ari.

"Tasha, are you all right? Come quickly, there is not much time."

Still sleepy and dazed she grabbed the candle and stood, then shook herself free and went back down the steps. "Ari, wait, there is something..."

She felt for the rock, dislodged it, and removed the emerald. Com must know that the jewel would be hidden somewhere in the dungeon, and would search for it, probably before searching for her.

"Tasha!" Ari's voice was insistent.

She shoved the small packet into the top of her shoe and felt it settle into her instep, then she gathered her skirts and ran up the steps.

"How did you...?"

"Later. Follow me."

Ari picked up the body of the guard, unconscious, bound, and gagged, and rolled him down the steps into the dungeon. Then he pulled the door shut and threw the bolt.

A small lantern was burning on the table. Ari picked it up and turned, walking away from the pantry entrance.

Tasha glanced toward the open doorway and the stairwell beyond. "But Ari..."

Once again he interrupted her. "Quiet. Just come."

He led her to the back of the shelf-lined room. One bank of shelves was turned sideways, revealing a passageway.

Tasha started to speak, then thought better of it. Ari was in no mood for questions. She had seen that. Better just to follow and ask questions later. But how did he know of this tunnel? She had explored the house over and over and lived there all of her life, but had never seen this. How many more such hidden passages were there in the old house?

The passage was wide. Tasha stepped through the doorway and Ari reached back, closing the door. On this side that is what it looked like, an ordinary heavy door. Someone must have built it, not as a secret passage, but as a regular underground hallway. The shelves must have been built on later to conceal it. Perhaps that had been done during one of the wars in the distant past.

At one time the hall must have had regular use. Though now a haven for spiders, the floor paving had been worn smooth. The walls and ceiling were cut stone, fitted together with skill and firmly in place. It was nothing like the crumbling walls in the dungeon.

Ari moved swiftly down the passage and Tasha followed closely, nearly running to keep up. Her joints were stiff from sitting so long in the dampness, and once she stumbled. Ari never paused. The passageway might be hidden, but they had to emerge somewhere, and that place might be watched.

As they walked, Tasha noticed that the floor began to

slant upward, gently at first, then more steeply. Finally they came to another door. From the angle of ascent, Tasha figured that they were now on ground level. She was right.

Ari opened the door, and they stepped into a small tack room. In this room as well, the door had been concealed by covering it with shelves and hooks for bits and bridles. They closed the door and Ari scattered and rearranged the straw on the floor that had been disturbed by its opening, and then he extinguished the lantern and hung it on a hook on the wall. A small window let in a bit of moonlight. It was enough for them to see their way.

Ari strode forward and carefully opened the other door of the tack room. It led into the stables where the best horses were kept. They moved swiftly past the ranks of stalls. Tasha breathed deeply, drinking in the smell of horseflesh, hay, and leather. But there was no time to contemplate old memories; already Ari was at the small entry door, waiting impatiently.

The courtyard was empty. Light still spilled out from the window of the house where the stable hands lived. There was the sound of laughter. A dog, roused from his sleep, ambled over to investigate their presence. Ari was ready with a low word and a bit of meat.

Ari seemed to glide across the courtyard. His soft-soled shoes made no sound. For Tasha it was more difficult. She wore high-topped shoes with hard leather heals and soles that clattered on the paving. Added to that was the difficulty of walking with the emerald in her shoe. By the time she crossed the open space and joined Ari in the shadows near the boathouse she was limping badly.

He didn't seem to notice. He just urged her on, skirting the edge of the lake, past the gazebo and kitchen gardens.

"Ari," Tasha's voice was a gasping whisper.

He paused only long enough to look behind him, then turned and waved for her to follow.

Tasha paused for a moment, took a deep breath, and then plunged on, determined that Ari would not find more cause to criticize her. It had been a foolish thing, going back for the jewel. But just as Ari had to exchange envelopes, she had to have that stone.

She glanced to her right. Across the water she could make out the piece of lawn where she had been sitting when she first met Marko. Fed by the river that surrounded the city, the lake shimmered in the moonlight. Rank and polluted under Com's careless rule, it still struck her with its beauty.

They passed the large vegetable garden and went through the little wicket gate into the lower orchard. A tree had fallen in a recent storm, mud still clung to the exposed roots. A large branch had broken off in the fall and lay on the ground. No attempt had been made to clean it up or salvage the wood.

There was no gate in the city wall on this side of the estate, but Tasha knew where Ari was headed. The lake was an artificial one and a sluice gate diverted the water from the Paulos River into a short channel under the city walls. The opening was covered with a grate, but some of the bars had broken off underwater, leaving enough space for a person to squeeze through. It was another one of those things that not many people knew about, but Tasha knew and so, it seemed, did Ari.

Ari waded into the water, dove down, and was through and under the wall before Tasha reached the edge of the stream. She jumped in, took a deep breath, and dove under the water. Her eyes burned from the drops of water that had splashed into them and she didn't dare open them to help find her way. She felt for the grate, fighting the current coming into the lake. She was too weak.

Coming to the surface she tried again. This time she swam until she was next to the grate, then, grasping the iron bars, she dove underwater and pulled herself down until she found the opening. She pushed herself through and fought her way to the surface. Ari was waiting, reaching out with a pole to help her into shore.

He waited a minute until she had caught her breath and had wrung some of the water from her heavy skirts, then turned on his heel and strode into the darkness of the woods.

The woods were unfamiliar to Tasha, and she was afraid she would lose him. She stumbled into the darkness, her eyes burning, her lungs still gasping for air.

Ari moved silently for a few minutes, and then turned around and motioned for Tasha to follow him the way they had come, back to the Paulos River. *Not this again!*

she thought, remembering the night they had left the compound.

This time Ari re-entered the water just below the cement sluice that fed the lake. He walked a few yards downstream in the shallows. There, from the shadows under the bank, he pulled out a boat. Helping her into the boat, he steered it out into the middle of the river, into the current. The spring floods, never too bad in this part of the country, were past and the current was sluggish. Ari rowed hard, and it was not long until they had left the city far behind them.

Tasha sat shivering in the boat. She had given up trying to wring any more water out of her skirts. Vaguely she wondered why they were following the river south. Finally Ari paused for a minute in his rowing, looked at her, and then reached behind him. He pulled out a blanket and tossed it to her. Still he did not speak. Tasha was too tired to care. She pulled the blanket around her shoulders, slid down onto the hull, rested her arms on the seat, and tried once more to sleep.

XX

"TASHA!" ARI'S VOICE WOKE HER. "TASHA, THE WATER IS shallow here, jump out of the boat!"

Tasha looked at him dumbly. But the boat was making good time. Why did they have to leave? She opened her mouth to speak, but in the light of early dawn, she could see it would be useless.

"Quickly, Tasha."

She hitched the blanket higher around her neck and shoulders, gathered her skirts as best she could, and stepped out of the boat into the shallow water of the river. Ari grabbed their packs from behind his seat and followed her with a soft splash. Wordlessly, he handed her one of the packs, then threw the oars into the water, and flipped the boat over. Another pack and an extra blanket bobbed to the surface. Tasha reached for them but Ari put out his hand and shook his head. They floated down the river with the boat.

In the distance downstream, Tasha could hear a soft rumble. She turned, listening to the noise. Ari answered her unspoken question. "Waterfall. The boat will break up on the rocks below. The river here is not swift, but the fall is high."

He led her to a rocky shelf and helped her out of the water. Once more he plunged into the woods. Now she was fully awake. Her stomach ached from want of food, and her mouth felt as if it were filled with cotton. Still, she pushed on, determined to keep up. She adjusted the blanket, picked up her skirts, and followed him.

They were headed east toward the faint pink of the sunrise. The woods were still dark, but the growing light helped them to find their way. Tasha tried to shut out the pain from the stone in her shoe. Why hadn't she taken it out when she was sitting in the boat?

"Because," she thought, "any normal person would have stayed with the boat and continued down the river to the seaport. Portaging around a waterfall is not as hard as walking all the way across country."

But Ari wasn't any normal person. He had his own ways, his own standards, his own thoughts. And right now, she was at his mercy.

Finally Tasha saw a small hunting cabin. The clearing was barely big enough for it to fit in. Built of logs, it blended in with the surroundings so perfectly that she would probably have missed it if she had been alone. She only saw it because Ari abruptly changed direction and walked toward it.

He was clearly impatient to be inside, but still he made her wait in the shadows and checked it out before he motioned for her to go in.

Ari ducked under the low doorway and tossed his pack into a corner. Tasha could stand her thirst no longer. She fumbled inside her pack for the water bottle and drank.

The water was not cold, but it was the sweetest thing Tasha had ever tasted. She took several large gulps, and then Ari reached out and gently took the bottle away from her.

"Don't drink too much. It will make you ill. I'm sorry. I should have known they would give you no water."

Tasha shrugged off his apology. "It was my fault I was caught. I should not have gone back upstairs."

"The papers?"

"I got them out and Angelino's boy got them fine. But I had to go back."

"Why, Tasha? What was so important?"

Tasha bent over and unlaced her shoe. She pulled out the little bundle. The cloth was covered with blood where the small diamonds surrounding the emerald had cut through the cloth and into the sole of her foot.

She unwrapped the jewels and held them out. "This."

"A jewel? You would jeopardize our entire mission and your life for a stone? Tasha, it is very beautiful and very valuable, but it isn't worth your life! It isn't worth risking everything for something like that!"

"Oh, isn't it? This belonged to my mother. It was a gift from my father. And what about you? You would risk all for what? A piece of paper in an envelope. You ask me to risk my life for it and then you don't even tell me what it is! This, Ari"—she held up the gem to the light, her hand shaking—"this is more than just a gem. It is all I have from my father and mother. It is like holding a piece of their love..."

The tears rose hot in her eyes, and she struggled to speak around the lump in her throat. "Of all that Com has taken, I couldn't let him have this too!" She turned her head. "Oh, never mind. You wouldn't understand."

Tasha closed her fingers over the sparkling warmth of the emerald, flung the blanket from around her shoulders, lay down on the rough bunk, and pulled the blanket up over her head.

"Tasha, I..."

"Forget it, Ari." Her voice was muffled by the blanket. "We're both too tired."

Tasha heard Ari's footsteps cross the floor. There was the scrape of the bolt being drawn, then the soft thud as he closed the shutters and locked them. The bunk on the other side of the room groaned as he settled himself, and soon she could hear his breathing, deep and regular, as he slept.

She lay quietly for a long time, but sleep would not come. Finally she rose and quietly removed her other shoe and her wet stockings. Her dress was nearly dry except for the hem, which had been wet again when they stepped out of the boat. She walked over to Ari's pack and started searching it.

The biscuits and jerky reminded her how hungry she was, but she refused to touch them. She sat down on the bench and felt her anger rising again like a red wave inside. Anger at herself for getting caught. Anger at Ari for his dictatorial attitude and lack of understanding. Anger at Marko for escaping when she could not. Anger at her father for his untimely death. And most of all, anger at Com for his treachery, his lies, his greed. He and his friends had devoured the entire nation, ruining everything they touched.

She became aware that her hands were clenched tight and the jewels were again cutting into her skin. Taking a deep breath, she set the emerald aside and continued to examine the pack. Finally she found what she was looking for, a needle and thread.

She no longer had the knife Ari had given her. It was confiscated when she was searched. Ari's knife lay in its sheath around his waist. She took it out. He stirred but did not wake. She cut a strip from the full skirt and folded it around the jewel, making a pocket. Then she covered herself with the blanket, slipped the dress off and sewed around all four sides of the pocket, securing it inside the bodice just above the waist. Refastening her buttons she threw off the blanket and sewed up the spot where she had cut out the material.

Carefully she put back the needle and thread. Ari had turned in his sleep and she could not replace the knife in the sheath, so she left it sitting on the bench.

Her hand wandered to the hard stone at her waist. She stretched, picked up the bottle of water, and took another long drink. They had made it this far. Com could not stop them now. The tension drained from her body and she was suddenly exhausted. She crossed the room and sank down on the hard bunk.

As she closed her eyes, Marko's face flashed through her mind. He was standing on the bank of a river, waiting and watching. Raina was there, running down the opposite bank, reaching and trying to get across to her brother. Ari was on the bank beside Raina. He was throwing a rope across to Marko. As she slipped into a deeper sleep the impression stayed in her mind. Ari had the rope. She must trust him to get them across the river.

XXI

ARI WAS NOT IN THE CABIN WHEN TASHA AWOKE. The knife was gone, but his pack was still there. Her water bottle had been refilled and was sitting on the small table in the middle of the room. Some biscuits and jerky and some fresh wild onions had been laid out as well.

Tasha poured out a little of the water to wash her hands and face and then sat down to eat. She ate slowly, savoring every bite. Where Ari had gone she did not know, but she was not worried. If he was still angry and had left her, then she would just have to make it on her own.

She picked up Ari's pack and searched it again. There was a map, more detailed than the one she had had in the cave. It was easy to follow their route down the Paulos River to where they had left the boat above the falls, a few miles north of the city of Fallgate. From there she could only guess where they went, and how far they had come.

They had gone east and probably a little north because the sunrise was in front and a little to their right as they hiked.

This patch of woods was not particularly large. It and the falls had once been part of a small national forest, but it was now labeled as a "hunting preserve." No doubt reserved for Com and his friends.

Tasha was sitting with her back to the door studying the map. She felt, rather than heard, Ari enter. There was a slight puff of fresh air and then his presence behind her.

"Thank you, Ari for the food and water. The onions were delicious."

He moved around and sat on the other side of the table. "You're welcome. I want to apologize for last night. I did not know your feelings for the emerald."

Tasha shook her head. "Even feeling as I do, I should not have gone back. How did you know where I was?"

"The housekeeper sent Samuel's grandson to find me. Samuel started to come after he gave you the candle, but was stopped by Com and his guards. Fortunately he told Old Sally where I was and she passed it on."

"Com told me they had stopped Samuel. Is he all right?"

"He was when we left. What Com will do when he finds out you're gone is anyone's guess. He can't blame Samuel; he was in his house under guard. Old Sally and the housekeeper and Ana were told to be together in a public place with lots of other people, far away from the house, before I got there. I will assume that they were. So it will be hard for any of them to be blamed."

"The guard at the door?"

"Just a knock on the head. He should be all right. He was watching the doorway and stairs. He didn't know about the service tunnel from the stables."

"How did you know? I'm sure Marko couldn't have told you, because I don't think Marko knows of its existence either. I have explored that house for years, but never knew of that place."

Ari smiled. "I told you I know that house better than you would suppose. Your father and I found that tunnel one rainy day when we were exploring. Only we entered from the stables. That door is not as well concealed as the other one, but few people go into that small tack room."

"My father?"

"Oh, Tasha, don't you know, even now?" Ari leaned forward, clasped his hands and rested his arms on the table. "I am Alexander."

"Alexander? My father's brother? But he has been dead for years!"

"I left home and renounced any rights to the throne that might come to me if anything happened to your father. My father was not pleased. I suppose to him I *was* dead. Your father knew, but I told him to just let things stay as they were. I did come back and sign the letter of abdication. My signature is only on the original, not on any copies, which is why it was important that we obtain the original from the compartment."

"Then it was you who stood back in the shadows that

night when father placed the letter in the compartment."

"I was there. I left again that night, and no one but your father and Old Samuel would have ever known, except for the war. Soon after the death of your father, when Com first started the rebellion, I returned and met with Marko. It was vital that he know Com's claim to royal birth was false."

"But how could Com have any claim to the throne?"

"He said he was my son."

"Of course! He told me last night that he ruled by right as son of my father's brother."

"His claim is false. His father was my best friend for many years until he died. There was an accident. I was injured too. Com and his mother left me for dead and traveled to the Capital, claiming that Com was my son. His father would never have tolerated such a thing, but his mother was always scheming."

There was the howl of a dog in the distance. Ari was instantly on his feet. "Grab your things; the searchers are approaching down the river."

Tasha dived for her shoes and socks and started to pull them on. "They have dogs. We can't get away."

"That is a signal from a friend. If they had left the river he would have shot into the air." Ari grabbed both packs, and Tasha took her blanket and the map.

Tasha's shoes were still damp, but the stockings were dry. Her foot was tender from the cuts, but the rest and food had refreshed her and she found she was full of energy.

She expected Ari to run, but though he moved quickly and quietly through the woods, his moves were deliberate and calculated. She did her best to match her shorter stride to his. He stepped always where a footprint would be least likely to show as he made his way through the dappled shadows.

Their path led them to a public road. This afternoon it was filled with people returning to their homes from the celebration of the day before. They merged in with the traffic heading south, walking behind a large wagon. Ari left her there for a while, walking ahead to where there was a string of farm wagons.

When he returned a few minutes later he took Tasha by the arm and hurried her forward, then helped her into the back of one of the middle wagons. The tailgate was off, and it was easy to hop up and sit in the back. Several families were returning to their village, a ride of a day and a half. Ari reached into his pocket and tossed Tasha a large kerchief for her to tie on her hair.

There were several people in the wagon, and Tasha and Ari gradually made their way back until they were sitting near the middle. Once a group of soldiers rode down the stream of people. Tasha kept her head down and the soldiers never stopped.

Near dusk the group stopped at a campground near a crossroad. Ari and Tasha got down from the wagon and merged in with a smaller group heading east. The people were tired and in no mood for conversation so it was easy just to walk along and not talk.

They entered another wooded area, and in a while a forest track turned off to the north. Ari briefly nodded his head, and Tasha moved to the side of the road to re-tie her shoe. When the last wagon and horseman had passed they slipped into the shadows and headed north up the narrow trail.

Ari passed her a biscuit and some jerky, and they ate as they walked.

They didn't talk. Their earlier conversation had given Tasha plenty to think about. Their anger and impatience with each other was gone, replaced with their old friendliness. But now there was something more for Tasha. This was no longer the Ari she had traveled with, a stranger, a wanderer, and Marko's friend. This was Alexander, the uncle she never knew, a man returned from the dead as far as she was concerned, for she had never thought of him as being alive. Over and over again she pictured the scene, her father as a young boy, exploring the house with his little brother and happening upon the long-forgotten service tunnel.

What else had the two boys shared together? How did they feel toward each other? Why had he left home, never to return? Com was not his son, but claimed to be. Why? Was there a son of Ari's somewhere? Or did he too die in the accident, whatever it was?

Still Ari strode into the darkness. His many years in the wilds seemed to give him an extra sense. Before they were visible, it seemed, he would move aside off the path to avoid mud holes or stretches where exposed rocks would make walking difficult. Once he moved silently into the trees, and Tasha followed without knowing why. They stood for a long time in the shadows, until a man on horseback passed, riding toward the south. They waited until he was far out of sight, before Ari moved out and once more followed the path northward.

Whether it was because she was energized by what Ari had told her, or because finally they were truly on their way, Tasha could not tell, but she did not feel tired. She focused her attention on following Ari's footsteps as closely as she could.

It took four days of travel, following a detour that led them far to the east of the Capital, before they approached the farm of Marta and Amoz near Elmore. It was as Ari feared. Troops surrounded the farm. Friendly neighbors told him that no one was being allowed in or out of the property immediately surrounding the house. Marta and Amoz and their children, together with Gil, Raina, and the farmworkers, were prisoners in their own home.

XXII

THEY MADE CAMP IN A SMALL CABIN BELONGING TO one of the members of the underground. It was in a back corner of his farm, hidden in a stand of trees. Ari paced the floor nervously, wanting to be gone, unable to leave the children, worried that they might have been discovered.

"Ari, please! I cannot think with you pacing like that."

"And I can't sit still with those soldiers swarming all over Amoz's farm."

"Well, it won't do any good to wear a path in the floor. Just say what you're thinking, that it's my fault that we were discovered. It's because of me the soldiers were sent." Tasha buried her head in her hands.

Ari knelt in front of her and gently took her by the shoulders.

"No, Tasha. You must not blame yourself. You did only

what you had to do, as I did what I felt had to be done. We—"

A soft knock on the door silenced him. Tasha rose from her chair and shrank into the shadows on the far side of the room. Ari, his knife drawn, approached the door. Through a crack he was able to see who was there.

"Gil!" Ari flung open the door with a strangled cry, pulling the boy inside.

"Oh, Gil"—Tasha rushed forward to embrace him— "How did you get out? How did you know we were here? What about Raina? Is she all right? Did she come with you?"

Laughing, Gil raised his hand. "I was out helping to bring the cows in from the pasture the day the soldiers came. It was about dusk, and it was easy to slip into a ravine and hide. I don't think they ever saw me."

Ari led the boy to a bench behind the table and then sat in a chair at its head. "Where have you been living?"

"A lot of woods around here aren't really part of any-one's farm. Ben was with me when we saw the soldiers. They've only been here for a couple of days. He told me about the farmer who owns this cabin, and that he would help me. I contacted him, but I've been living in the woods. I've been eating the greens and cattails you told me were safe. I even snared a rabbit yesterday."

Tasha, seated at the foot of the table, reached out and took his hand. "But how did you know we were here?"

"With soldiers around, I figured you got the papers you wanted and would be along. The farmer said he would put two lamps in his window and try to get you to come here when you arrived."

"And Raina?"

"She fits into that family like a pea in a pod. She's all right. There was a green shirt on the clothesline this morning. I could see it when I climbed a tree overlooking the farm. They hang it out every day that everyone is all right. We thought something might happen, so Ben and I decided on a signal." Gil grinned. "I bet that's the cleanest shirt in the country."

"So"—Ari leaned back in his chair, his face alight with pride—"have you two figured out a way to get Raina out of there?"

Gil cocked his head to one side. "Of course we have. And Com gave it to us just last week."

He reached inside his shirt and drew out an official-looking letter.

It was on parchment, sealed with Com's own seal.

"When this came we didn't know what it was, but we thought it might prove useful, so we never broke the seal. Marta just slipped a hot knife under it to open the letter. It's an order for dried beans, pickles, and wheat. Com likes to give farmers the privilege of 'donating' to his cause."

"So," Tasha asked, "how does this help us?"

"I kept the order since I would have the best chance of getting away if something happened, which it did.

The farmer here said he would lend me a wagon. I'll just go down tomorrow morning with the wagon, collect the order and Raina, and bring everything out past the guards."

"But they're sure to search the wagon."

"Of course, but I don't think they'll dump out an entire barrel of good dried beans meant for his majesty onto the ground. After chores were done, Ben and I made some modifications in a couple of the storage barrels. Some of them won't hold very many beans at all, but there's plenty of room under the false bottom to hide a child like Raina."

Ari shook his head. "You two seem to have thought of everything."

"Of course." Gil gave Ari a nudge with his elbow. "I inherited a great brain."

Ari smiled and then sobered as his chair came down with a thump.

"This will be very dangerous. If you are discovered, not only will you and Raina suffer, but so will Marta, Amoz, and all of their children."

"I know. But the longer Raina stays there, the greater the chance that she will be found out." He turned to look at Tasha. "She's been doing great, but she misses you something fierce. She stays inside a lot so that people won't start counting heads and find an extra. She'll be glad to come.

"I'm going to signal Ben tonight that we're ready. At dawn I'll pick up the team and wagon, and in a few hours she should be out."

"Who is going to make the delivery?" Ari asked. "Com will be expecting his order."

"The farmer who has the wagon also has a son. He's been wanting a little excitement. He'll take it on into the Capital."

"And if the soldiers decide to escort you?"

"I don't think they will. They're too busy watching the farm. If they do, then a group of starving peasants will just have to steal a barrel of beans to last them until their crops come in next fall."

Gil slid off the bench and started for the door. "I'd better get the signal up for Ben."

"Just a minute, Gil." Ari reached out and took hold of his arm. "I think it would be better if we waited for you in the hills, away from the farm. There is another cave the underground has used. It isn't far. Ben knows the way."

"So do I." Gil smiled again. "Ben and I went on a hike and 'discovered' it. Just in case anything should happen."

"Gil, wait!" Tasha grabbed her pack and started rummaging around in it. She pulled out the small packet of bone hairpins that she had brought from the compound.

"Give these to Ben. Tell him to give them to his mother when we are well away. She'll recognize them." She glanced at Ari. "I need her to know I have come this far safely."

Tasha pressed the packet into Gil's hand. "Thank you, Gil. Please be careful."

Gil flashed a grin, gave Ari a salute, and stepped out the door.

At dusk Ari and Tasha started for the cave. They reached it well before daylight. The night was clear, and starlight brightened their path. Once inside the cave they settled down in a small room off the main tunnel, not bothering to go farther back. It was cool and the blankets were welcome, but the floor was dry sand and Tasha, in spite of her concern over Raina and Gil, soon fell asleep.

When she awoke Ari was gone. She arose and felt her way to the main tunnel. From the angle of light that penetrated the entrance, she assumed it must be late afternoon. Back in the cave she could see the reflection of a fire. Using it as a guide, she made her way back to another small room. Ari had uncovered some of the supplies the underground had stashed and was busy cutting up vegetables to make another pot of his nourishing stew. Tasha settled herself near the fire, grateful for the warmth.

"The children may be hungry when they arrive," Ari said.

For a while Tasha sat silently, hugging her knees. Finally the question inside her refused to be silent any longer. "Why did you leave?"

"Leave?" Ari seemed puzzled at the question.

"Your home. Why did you leave your home and Grandfather?"

Ari shrugged. "Government was for your father, not for me. I could barely stand to stay indoors during school time. I couldn't face a lifetime of hearing complaints, making laws, negotiating with one faction and another. I wanted the freedom of a simple life. I just left."

"And Grandfather was not pleased." It was more a statement than a question.

"No, he was not pleased. To him, I was abandoning my responsibility. But, I was young. His displeasure was easy to ignore."

"But where did you go?"

"North. I came the way we are going now. Eventually I stopped in the small fishing village of Kershaw a few miles up the coast from where the Great North River enters the ocean. For several years I worked on fishing boats, until I earned enough to buy my own."

"But surely you had enough money with you to do that."

"When I left, I renounced everything, including my inheritance." He held out his hands to the firelight. They were rough and calloused, sinewy and strong. "What I had, I wanted to earn with my own two hands. I wanted to be measured against myself, not on the shoulders of someone else."

He picked up the wooden spoon and stirred the stew. "With my own boat, I knew I could provide well. I married the daughter of the innkeeper. We were very happy, but her father was furious."

"But, why? Why would he object?"

"He wanted her to marry above her station, to better herself in life. He did not fancy a fisherman as a son-in-law. Lydia begged me to tell him who I really was, but I refused. I wanted to be accepted for myself, not for my father. In trying to be humble, I was too proud."

He dropped the spoon and stared at the glowing coals. "We had a son. I built her the largest house in the village. If we had had more time, her father might have softened. I bought another boat and took on Com's father, Josef, as a partner. Com and my son were nearly the same age. They played together, our wives became friends. That is how, I think, that Com's mother found out the truth of who I was. Lydia must have confided in her."

"And the accident?"

"There was a storm. I made it in to shore safely. Josef had the two boys out on his boat that day. They were about ten. The fishing boat was driven onto some rocks at the entrance of the bay. I went back out for them in a rowboat. A large wave capsized the boat as we neared the shore. Only Com and I made it in alive."

Ari picked up a stick, broke it, and threw it into the fire. The flames flared up, highlighting his white hair. His blue eyes were dark with sorrow.

"Our second son was only a few days old. The labor and delivery had been very hard on Lydia. I was badly injured and could not help her. She contracted childbed fever. Com's mother took the baby and left him with Lydia's family. Then she took Com and disappeared.

"When I recovered I found that Lydia had died. Her family is large, and was very wealthy. They hid my son from me, moving him whenever I came too close to finding out where he was. I sold everything, gave the money to the bank to hold in trust for the baby, and became a wanderer, never really giving up the search. I knew I could identify him by the birthmark on his back. I hoped they would raise him as one of their own. Instead they treated him as a servant."

He picked up another stick and poked at the coals until the end began to blaze. "Com's mother took with her the birth record of my older son. They were so close in age. She tried to use it to claim an inheritance for him at court."

"Did Father believe her?"

"We always stayed in touch. He had even met Lydia, so he knew Com's mother was an impostor. He sent a message to me. As soon as I could I traveled to Elmore. We met at the home of Amoz and Marta. Your father was even then finalizing his plans for abdication. Since there was to be no kingdom to inherit, we decided to let things remain as they were. Com would be given a chance for an education with the other boys, but nothing would ever be said about his mother's claim. I went back to locate Com's true birth record."

"The other envelope."

"Yes. Your father put the one containing the birth record of my son into the secret compartment. I located the other one, but we were never able to make the switch."

"Until now," Tasha said.

"Yes, until now." A fleeting smile passed over Ari's face. "Com believes that somewhere in that house is his claim to the throne, false as it is. When he discovers the papers have been switched, I do not think he will be pleased."

"So, that was what Father meant by the message."

"What message?"

"The day he died. It wasn't long after Marko's inauguration that Com started to court influential men who lost power in the switch to democracy. Father suspected he was laying the foundation for a return to the monarchy. He wanted to talk to Com alone so he arranged to take him on a hunting trip."

Tasha stood and walked to the other side of the fire, her back stiff. "A wolf pack had moved into a den too near the village of Ashdon. A lot of farmers were complaining about their sheep being killed. Father and Com came upon the den unexpectedly and surprised the cubs. Their cries brought the pack. Both horses were attacked. Com was thrown and nearly trampled. His shoulder and arm were broken and his leg twisted so he could barely walk. Father's horse reared up and kept going, all the way over backward. Com was able to finally chase the wolves away, but he could not save Father. He was injured inside. A woodsman helped Com make arrangements to bring Father home. He died the day after they arrived."

"And the message?"

"The doctor let me in to see him. He said, 'I didn't get a chance. Tell Com it's no use, give it up. Com's mother, it was a lie. We know the truth.'"

She turned and knelt in front of the fire, seeking its warmth.

"Then he lost consciousness. Just before he died he opened his eyes long enough to tell me of his love. And that was all. I gave Com the message. It disturbed him, but when he realized I didn't know what it meant, he seemed relieved. I never tried to find out. But with Father gone, Com moved faster. You know the rest."

Ari stood and gathered an armful of wood from the other side of the room. He carried it to the fire and poked the sticks under the simmering pot. "I never knew the details, only that there had been a hunting accident. I should have returned sooner and more openly, instead of meeting privately with Marko. Perhaps I could have blocked Com and kept him from taking over."

"I don't think any of us knew how far along Com was with his plans. He thinks that Marko deceived Father and talked him into giving up the throne. He says bringing back the monarchy is his way of honoring Father's memory. He didn't realize that the power itself would corrupt him."

Tasha looked at Ari. How could she have ever missed the resemblance? His eyes had always reminded her of her father's, but now she could see him in Ari's every movement. She shivered with the sudden coldness of fear. She looked into his face. "Does Com know you are alive?"

"I think he suspects, but I do not think he knows for sure. If he saw me, I believe he would remember me."

"But surely he knows you are not his father."

"Com was a small child when his father died. His father and I lived the same kind of life. Of those in the village, only Lydia and Com's mother knew my true identity. If his mother said that it was his father who was living a concealed life and was next in line to the throne, who would he be to question her? After he grew to know your father, I'm sure he realized that his mother was lying, that I was heir, not Josef. But by then he wanted the throne too much to let go of the lie."

There was a stirring at the entrance to the cave. Ari pulled out his knife, and Tasha moved away from the fire. A cautious whisper broke the silence.

"Ari?"

"Gil?" Ari fired a torch and moved out into the tunnel. "Do you have her?"

"Yes. Come, Raina, Tasha is here."

Tasha stumbled forward, catching the child in her arms.

XXIII

THEY LEFT AS SOON AS THEY HAD CLEANED UP FROM their supper. The night was clear and bright, and it was not hard to find their way. Raina had spent most of the day curled up inside the barrel and was glad for the chance to run and stretch.

Before they left the cave, Ari handed Tasha and Raina each a pair of trousers and a shirt of sturdy homespun. "Wear these," he said. "You can walk more quickly if you are not hampered by long skirts."

There was a small pocket sewed onto the pants he gave to Tasha. "For the jewel," he said. "Here is a needle and thread. Sew the opening shut securely. You don't want to have to worry about it." Tasha gave him a grateful smile and took the clothes.

As she returned to the fire after changing, Ari was putting on his leather vest as if he too had changed. He looked up and smiled.

"Gil has done some good work." He clapped the boy on the shoulder. "I told Angelino to try to get the papers to him. Angelino contacted the underground, and the farmer who owned the cabin got word to Gil. He met one of the boys after their performance in Elmore, took the packets, and hid them in that passageway over there. They are here." He patted a bulge at his waist. "If anything happens to me, Tasha, you must make sure these papers get to Marko."

With that he turned and led the way out of the cave.

Once again they traveled by night, sleeping during the day in hidden ravines or seldom-visited cabins Ari knew about, tucked into thick patches of woods.

The rolling hills and broad valleys gave way to a steep coastal mountain range. They were the final barrier standing between them and the river crossing. On the other side of the Great North River were Marko and his band of freedom fighters, waiting at the Camp of the Exiles.

It was slower traveling in the steeper terrain. Tasha noticed that, while Raina often walked beside her, holding her hand, when she grew tired she turned to Gil. Playfully he would squat down while she climbed onto his back, twining her legs around his waist. He would carry her piggyback for miles. He never complained, nor asked to be relieved of his burden. Ari watched them closely, and when he saw that Gil was starting to get too tired, he would call a halt and they would rest, snacking on jerky, nuts, or dried fruit.

Small caches of food had been placed along their route.

Whether they had been put there by members of the underground, or whether Ari himself had left them on his trip to the compound, Tasha did not know. It was not important and it was better to save one's breath for the effort of the journey.

After the fifth night of travel, they emerged at sunrise into a high mountain valley. The green carpet of spring grass was studded with wildflowers. A doe and her fawn were drinking from a small beaver pond that had diverted a mountain spring in its headlong rush toward the valley floor.

A house with neat outbuildings stood at the edge of the meadow. No hunter's cabin this. The breaking rays of sunshine glinted off glass windows hung with crisp white curtains, giving it a lived-in look. Still, everything was too quiet and undisturbed, as if the family had sunk into a magical sleep.

Tasha gasped in surprise as the house came into view. "They're gone," Ari said, answering her unspoken question. "They had plans in place to leave when I came through on my way to the compound, but were just waiting for word. They should be across the river now, with Marko."

Tasha felt a surge of elation, knowing that this family, who obviously loved their home so much, loved their country and their freedom still more. Enough so that they were willing to leave what they had and join with Marko.

Ari spoke, as if he had read her thoughts. "There are many like this who have left all they have. More leave every day. Even the soldiers who are sent to guard the borders sometimes slip away in the night and make their way to Marko. Many others are like Amoz. They show a smiling face to Com, but behind their back each has a dagger waiting."

They skirted the lower end of the valley and came to a spring above the beaver pond. Ari shed his pack. "Fill your water bottles from here," he said. "It is the sweetest water in the country."

Ari led them to a small log house in the upper end of the valley. More than just a hunting cabin, it boasted three rooms and a loft. "The family lived here before they built the other house," Ari explained. "They keep it furnished and ready for visitors."

The loft was divided into two rooms, and Raina quickly scrambled up the ladder to claim one while Gil took the other. Tasha was grateful for the privacy of a real bedroom. Ari slept on a small cot that was pushed up in a corner of the large living room.

It was still early afternoon when Tasha awoke to a knock on the bedroom door. Ari stood there with a large galvanized tub. Behind him were Gil, lugging a large pail of water, and Raina, holding a steaming teakettle.

"We thought you might like a bath, Tasha," Raina said as they trooped in, deposited the tub, and filled it.

"A bath! And even with warm water!" Tasha gave Raina a hug. "M-m-m. I think someone else has had a bath too!"

"Oh yes. And so did Gil and Ari, but I had to play upstairs in my room with the door shut until they were finished. Now Ari says Gil and I can go outside to play."

Tasha looked at Ari. "Is it safe?"

"I doubt any soldiers will come looking here. This place is fairly isolated. If anyone comes, they will probably give plenty of warning. The children will be watchful and should be fine."

"All right." Tasha paused and took Gil by the arm. "Thank you Gil, for all you have done for Raina."

The boy blushed, not knowing what to say.

Raina interrupted, "Gil's my big brother. Come on, let's go outside and play." She grabbed his hand and headed for the door.

Tasha shut the door and started to get ready for her bath. The sunlight streamed in through the half-curtained windows, but suddenly Tasha felt inexplicably cold. She hurried through her bath, hardly noticing the sweet smelling soap or the lovely feeling of clean hair.

Tasha dressed and opened the door into the big room. Ari was sitting on the stoop, working with some leather. The door was open to the warm breeze. She looked around for a pail that she could use to dip out the water when a scream from Raina split the air. Gil was yelling, too. "No, no, get away from her!"

Instantly Ari was on his feet, his knife in his hand running toward the undergrowth at the edge of the woods. Tasha followed, honing in on the sound of the little girl's cries. She didn't see the tree root in her path and fell headlong. In an instant she was up again. Ari had vanished into the bushes.

Gil cried again, this time an unearthly scream of pain. There was a shout from Ari, and as Tasha forced her way through the twigs and branches, she caught a glimpse of a dark shape retreating into the woods.

They were in a small clearing, made larger by the trampled bushes. The children had been picking wild strawberries that had ripened early. A small pail lay on the ground, the red fruit spilling over the carpet of green. But there was other red, too. The red of blood. Gil lay on the ground. Blood poured from wounds on his back and head. Ari had stripped off his own shirt and was working frantically, using shreds of the cloth to stem the flow.

Raina was hysterical and flung herself at Tasha. "Tasha!...a bear...the berries. His teeth...Gil hit him."

"We need to get Gil inside. Get some water boiling to clean his wounds." Ari picked up the boy and started for the house, heedless of the branches that tore at his bare flesh.

Tasha dumped the remaining berries from the pail and ran toward the spring, still holding Raina. The little girl sobbed into her neck as they ran.

A fire was burning in the stove and the teakettle, emptied for Tasha's bath, had been refilled and was simmering on the back. Tasha set down the pail of water and grabbed a shawl off the back of an old rocking chair. Wrapping it tightly around Raina, she set the child down in the chair and searched the cupboards for a clean basin.

There was one under the sink. She emptied the teakettle into the basin and then refilled it from the pail.

Snatching up some dishtowels and a bar of strong lye soap lying on the counter, she entered the living room. Ari stripped off the boy's clothing and gently bathed his wounds with the scalding water. Tasha ripped the towels, rolled them into bandages, then went for more water. Again and again she threw out the basin of bloody water and filled it from the steaming kettle. Finally there was no more they could do.

Tasha found a clean shirt for Ari and draped it around his shoulders. He put it on automatically, his eyes never leaving Gil's still form.

Gil was in shock, his face pale, his skin cold and clammy. Once he woke and called for Raina. The little girl crept in and sat beside him, holding his hand, her tears mingling with her kisses on his cheek.

Near sunset he opened his eyes and looked for Ari. "The bear," he said. "The bear was going to attack Raina. Ari, I couldn't let it hurt her."

Ari caressed the boy's hand. "You did the right thing, Gil. I'm proud of you."

At Ari's words the boy's eyes lit up, then closed again as he slipped back into unconsciousness.

Gradually the cabin grew dark. Tasha sat on the floor between the wall and the cot, holding Raina, who refused to let go of Gil's hand. Ari, on the other side, sat on a small stool, holding his other hand, wiping his brow, talking to him in a low voice, sometimes coaxing him to take a small sip of water. Finally, Tasha dozed, aware only of the ache in her back, Raina's weight on her lap, and the soft murmur of Ari's voice.

"Gil! No!" The cry broke from Ari's throat like that of a wild animal. He rose, kicking the stool backward across the room and rushed into the night.

Tasha, startled awake by the sound, hugged Raina more tightly to her. The little girl was crying again. Tasha reached out and took the boy's hand. It was still warm, but there was no pulse in the wrist. Gently she tucked the hand under the blanket, then carried Raina into the bedroom and shut the door.

She took off her shoes and Raina's, then tucked the child into bed beside her. Raina sobbed herself to sleep. Tasha lay there, staring into the darkness.

Finally Ari returned. She heard the scrape of the stool and knew he had once more taken his place beside the body of the boy. With Ari's return, she felt herself begin to relax. As the tension eased, the tears came, and Tasha, too, cried until she could cry no more. Then she slept.

The funeral was a simple one. There were pine boards in a curing shed, perhaps cut and ready for a new room. Ari took what he needed and made a coffin. Tasha found a patchwork quilt. Gently Ari wrapped Gil's still form in its brightness and laid him in the simple box. Tasha carried

Raina outside, but they could not help but hear the sound of the nails being pounded into the lid.

They buried him in a corner of the meadow where a forsythia bush spilled gold. Ari said a simple prayer and then turned to the task of replacing the mound of rich dark soil, while Tasha and Raina made their way back to the cabin.

XXIV

HERE WAS AN OUTCROPPING OF GRANITE NOT FAR from the edge of the meadow. A large boulder lay apart from the rest. This Ari moved to the grave. He spent the rest of the morning and most of the afternoon chiseling deep Gil's name, his birth date, and the day of his death.

"It's beautiful, Ari," Tasha said, tracing the letters with her fingers. "And it will last forever."

She paused and looked again. "You have only put his first name. He said you told him what his name was. Didn't you know his last name?"

Ari leaned against the rock. "He had no last name, Tasha. Just as you have no last name. Just as I have no last name."

"But only those of the house of my grandfather have no last name." She looked at him quizzically, then understanding dawned.

"Yes, Tasha. Gil was my son."

"Oh, Ari. The baby you were not allowed to see." She reached out and took his calloused hand.

Ari suddenly looked very old and very tired. He sat on a nearby stump. Tasha sat on the grass at his feet. "The cook at the compound was his grandfather, Lydia's father. He raised Gil, not as a grandson, but as a servant. Not until Com stripped him of his property and made him serve in the compound was he humbled enough to realize what he had done to the boy."

"So that is why he lead the searchers away."

"Yes, we had many long talks, he and I, in the first days after I arrived at the compound looking for you. In the beginning he refused to tell me anything about the boy, but after I identified Gil from the birthmark on his back, he no longer tried to keep us apart."

Ari lifted his eyes to gaze at the mountain peaks. "It wasn't until that day before we left Amoz's farm that Gil knew the whole truth. I told him then. I think he even forgave his grandfather, once he understood. He had always wanted a family. Raina became for him more of a sister than a friend. He loved her..." Ari's voice broke.

Tasha stood and touched him on the shoulder. "Yes, he loved her more than life. No one can love more." She walked toward the house, leaving him alone with his grief.

Later she passed the window and saw Raina, her arms full of wildflowers, kneeling in front of the stone. Ari helped her arrange them, then took the little girl in his arms and returned to the stump.

It was dusk before they entered the cabin to eat the food that Tasha had prepared from the stores in the kitchen. For a long time Raina was silent. Then she looked at Tasha, her eyes dry and solemn. "Tasha, please help me to be good, so that someday I can go and live with Gil again."

Tasha looked at Ari and then took the child's hand. "I'll try, Raina. I'll try very hard."

It was gray dawn when Tasha awoke the next morning. Ari was carefully pouring a little milk into each of three bowls of steaming cornmeal mush on the table.

"Milk?" Her voice was incredulous. "Where did you find milk?"

Ari shrugged. "The farmer left the nanny behind. She wandered back to the barn and was nosing around this morning. Her kids must be grown. She was glad to be rid of it."

After breakfast, Tasha washed the dishes and tidied up the cabin while Ari once more made up their packs. She looked out the window at the golden forsythia bush, the flower-strewn meadow, the forest of aspen and pine. In spite of their sorrow there was such peace here, such a feeling of safety. How tempting it would be to stay.

She bent down to tuck the covers around the mattress. The wooden dove dangled from its leather thong around her neck. She straightened and tucked it inside her dress. Again her eyes were drawn to the window, to the scar of raw earth with its granite marker.

Tasha picked up the small rug and stepped outside to

shake it. Ari was sitting on the stoop, Raina on his lap. His voice was low, quiet and kind, but there could be no misunderstanding the seriousness of what he was saying.

"From now on, little one, until we cross the river and meet your brother, you must be very strong and very quiet. Trust no one. Speak to no one unless I tell you it is all right. You are strong and must use that strength to help us. Tell me or Tasha if you see or hear anything unusual. Always tell us if you smell smoke. You are very important to us. Do not be afraid. We will keep you safe. Do you understand?"

Raina nodded solemnly, her eyes trusting.

Ari gave her thin shoulders a squeeze and then carefully removed her heavy shoes.

"I have a gift," he said. "For one who can remain as silent as the wind in the grass."

He reached down beside him and brought out two pairs of soft leather slippers. "These are for Tasha," he said, "but these are for you." He slipped the smaller pair on her feet.

The soles of both were made of cowhide, supple but strong to protect from rocks and sticks, the deerskin tops were high, and they were lined with fur for warmth. Tasha put her own pair on and understood at once why Ari preferred their light weight and comfort over heavy boots.

Ari carefully laced and tied the pair on Raina's feet. Carved into the top of each was the pattern of a dove, one in flight, one resting safely, its wings folded.

"Now," Ari said, pointing to the flying dove, "we are

like this dove, flying toward Marko. But soon," he added, pointing to the other, "soon you will be safe, like the dove in its nest."

Raina smiled, "Thank you," she whispered. She wrapped her arms tightly around his neck in a hug. "Thank you. I will try very hard."

"I know you will," Ari said gruffly. He set her down and stood. Cradling her face in his strong hands, he looked deep into her eyes. "You will do more than try. You will *do* it."

"Yes," she said, her voice full of faith and resolve. "I *will* do it."

She picked up her small pack. Tasha replaced the rug, set the broom in its corner, and latched the door. Holding hands, the three of them left the mountain meadow and started to climb toward the pass.

XXV

IT TOOK THEM A DAY AND A HALF TO REACH THE FINAL approach to the pass. Though they tried to avoid the main road, there were times when it was impossible. The terrain was rough and steep, and they were forced to use the road more and more. The going was slow. Again and again, they had to scramble into the brush or hide in a ravine to avoid passing patrols. They decided to cross the pass itself at night. Clouds, rain, and even snow were not unusual at this high elevation, and this night was no exception.

Rain was beginning to fall and the sky was dark when they left their final hiding place and started up the road. Only a small light, spilling out from a guard shack at the top of the pass, marked the way. Raina was exhausted, and Ari was carrying her in front of him. She clung tightly to his neck, her legs wrapped around his waist.

Silently they approached the shack. The noise of the storm muffled the sound of their passing. Staying close to the shadows, they passed the summit and started down the other side. The rain was cold, driven by a sharp wind. Still, it had kept patrols indoors and would cover their tracks.

On the other side of the mountain, the storm grew worse, driven by the wind from the sea. Finally Ari felt that they had gone far enough, and he found them shelter among some rocks in a stand of aspen and pine trees.

Tasha was so wet and miserable that she was sure she would not be able to sleep, but a swarm of gnats buzzing in her face startled her and she awoke to hot sun streaming down through the dripping trees. Brushing away the insects, she stretched her legs and moved to a spot on a rock that the sun had dried and warmed. How good it felt as the warmth penetrated her damp clothing.

Through a break in the trees she could see the river where it flowed into a great bay of the sea. She was surprised at its closeness. It was an anomaly, this river, running toward the north while all the others traveled south. The river was wide, nearly a mile across in some places, and it was hard to see the other side. So that was where they were going. Over there were her people, those for whom freedom was more important than their homes. Over there was Marko. She felt a stir of pleasure as she thought of seeing him again and how happy he would be to see Raina.

Ari awoke and came to sit beside her. "We will not cross so close to the bay. That is where the road leads. We must follow the cliffs south, to where the river bends. That is where our crossing is. That is where Marko will be waiting for us. They keep a constant watch for those who are trying to cross the river."

Tasha followed his pointing finger with her eyes, and it seemed she could make out a thin column of smoke on the far bank. Ari saw it too. "See, they are there, waiting for us. We will wait until the sun is a bit lower and the cliffs are in shadow. It won't take long, but we must be able to see. Otherwise the cliffs are too dangerous."

Raina was awake before it was time to leave. They ate a brief lunch, and then Ari stashed their packs behind a rock. "We won't need these now. They will only encumber us as we cross the river. When they see us coming they will send a boat, but we may have to swim for a while."

Quietly they made their way down the steep mountainside. Once Tasha slipped, setting off a small avalanche of rocks. Once they startled a mountain goat, and he went bounding away up the mountain. There was a sharp "boom" of a musket. Ari held up his hand and they stopped, shrinking against a boulder.

Then he smiled. "Someone will have goat stew for supper."

Still, it was a signal to all of them that patrols were out. Carefully they continued downhill.

They were near the head of a small trail that wound down toward the edge of the cliff. Ari untied the strings on his vest and picked up Raina, carrying her in front as he had done the night before. She wound her legs around his waist and locked her feet together, then clasped her hands around his neck. He motioned to Tasha, and she wrapped the vest around Raina, tying the leather thongs as tightly as she could. The vest would help support the child and leave his hands free for the climb down the cliff.

As they approached the trail they heard a shout behind them. A passing patrol had found their packs. Scrambling as fast as they dared down the steep hillside, they reached the trail just as they heard another shout and another "boom," followed by the thud of a musket ball as it hit a nearby boulder.

They reached the trail and started to run. A sharp outcropping of rock shredded the soles of Tasha's slippers. Her feet left a trail of blood. Ari's legs pumped beside her. They reached the edge of the cliff. The trail wound down the side, narrow and steep. Green willows lined the shore. She looked and saw a boat anchored in the middle of the stream. It appeared to be a fishing boat, but she knew instinctively that no fishermen were aboard.

Momentarily, the trail widened as it passed over an overhang. Tasha never felt the ball that slammed into her shoulder. She knew only that a giant hand had pushed her sideways and forward, off the face of the cliff. She looked toward the boat, then turned to see the panic in Raina's eyes as Ari jumped after her into space. Her stomach lurched, and she slumped forward into darkness.

Through a haze of light and dark, Tasha could hear a murmur of voices and the slap, slap of waves. Her clothes were wet, but the pillow under her head was soft. Someone was holding her hand and she could feel the gentle caress of a rough hand across her cheek. Raina was calling, but Gil was there too, standing between her parents. She struggled to open her eyes. The effort was too much, and she drifted off again into the dark.

It was the pain that finally woke her, a sharp, throbbing pain in her left shoulder and a dull ache in her feet and legs. Now her clothes felt clean and dry, and someone was gently bathing her feet. A murmur of voices ebbed and swelled through the room. The tone was so familiar. She relaxed into the softness surrounding her, not yet willing to open her eyes.

Bandages were wound around her feet, then ripped and tied around her ankles. The clean stockings felt delicious as they were pulled carefully up over the dressings.

A soft blanket, warmed by the fire, was tucked around her. She felt the rough hand holding her own. She somehow knew that that hand had always been there, pulling her back from the darkness, willing her to live.

She forced herself to concentrate on the voice. "... And

those poor feet. I daresay it will be a while before she will be up and around. It's a good thing that the little one finally was able to sleep. How you ever made it . . . oh my dear, sweet girl . . ."

Tasha opened her eyes, "Ana? Ana?" Fear rose inside her. Were they somehow back in the Capital? Back under Com's power?

She struggled to sit up, looking around wildly, then once more she relaxed. Ana was there, but so was Ari. Marko sat by the side of the bed, holding her hand and grinning broadly. His hazel eyes never left her face.

"Marko"—Tasha swallowed, trying to speak around the lump in her throat—"You're all right."

Marko squeezed her hand. "We've had several skirmishes. Often families need help in crossing the border. But yes, I'm all right."

Tasha caught her breath as a bubble of happiness rose through her, so sharp it was almost painful. Marko's blond curls appeared darker than she remembered, his shoulders and arms even broader and more muscular. Marko was not tall, but his solid strength seemed to flow through his hand into her own. She forced herself to turn away, startled at the depth of her feelings.

"Ana, how did you . . . ? I thought . . . ?"

"After your escape I just couldn't stay any longer. As soon as I could get away, I went to Bismire. Samuel's grandson helped me. We found someone willing to get us out to a ship that was going north to Oldom." Ana bent over and gave Tasha a quick kiss on the cheek.

Ari laughed. "You're lucky the rest of us were even allowed in the room. Ana has insisted in caring for you since we got to the camp."

Tasha looked around, "Raina?"

"Sleeping." It was Marko who spoke. "She wouldn't leave you. I was holding her, and we had to sit here beside you until she fell asleep." He gave her hand a gentle squeeze. "Thank you, Tasha, for caring for her."

There was a sudden burning in her eyes and Tasha blinked back the tears. "Gil..."

"I told them," Ari said.

"Yes," said Marko. "I wish I could have known him and thanked him."

Tasha glanced down at the bandages swathing her shoulder. "What happened? It felt as though someone pushed me."

"You were shot," Marko said. "The ball went right through your shoulder. You went down so fast, it may have helped save your life. You landed at the edge of the water. The water and willows broke your fall."

Pulling her hand away from Marko's grasp, she felt for the jewel at her waist.

"The emerald is safe," Ari said. "Ana took it and is keeping it for you." He looked at Ana and laughed again. "And I daresay not even Com himself could ever get that away from her."

"And the envelopes?"

"Safe as well," Marko said. "The council is studying them now. The ones Ari was able to get will prove invaluable when we launch our attack. The others, as you know, prove false any claim Com may have to rule."

Marko reached for a packet on the table. "Old Samuel's grandson gave this to me. He said it belonged to you."

It was the packet from the secret compartment. She raised herself up on her elbow. "Open it, Marko. I don't know what it is."

Carefully, Marko untied the bindings, then slipped a knife under the seal. It was a miniature, copied from the formal family portrait that had hung in the great hall. In spite of the stiff formality of the pose, the love was there, in the way her father rested his hand on her mother's shoulder, the way she laid her hand on his knee. Tasha was half turned, looking at her mother. Her hair rippled down her back.

"Your father's most valuable treasure, Tasha. His family." Marko carefully set the small painting on the table where she could easily see it.

Tasha sank back on the pillows and closed her eyes for a minute. Gradually she became aware of an ache in her left hand. She drew it out and painfully forced it to open. It was holding the little wooden dove.

"You must have grabbed it as you fell," Ari said. "You wouldn't let it go so we cut the thong and left it in your hand."

"The dove has flown." Tasha fingered the outstretched

wings, echoing Ari's words that he had first spoken in the cave so long ago.

Marko's eyes held Tasha's. "Since you left the compound, people have been arriving every day. Not just soldiers, but ordinary people, like Ana and the family who owned the house in the meadow."

He reached out and gently reclaimed her hand, holding it in both of his own. "You're here, Tasha, and the people have followed you, as they followed your father. For two years we have been waiting and preparing for the time when we would be strong enough to go back and face Com. Now, at last, we're ready."

Tasha leaned back on the pillows. There was so much still to do. She looked at Ari and saw again those eyes that were so much like her father's. They had the same dreams, Ari and her father. They approached them differently, but the dream was the same. Peace and freedom. She reached out and placed the necklace in Ari's hand. "Thank you."

Then Tasha closed her eyes and slept.